REDBI

To renew this it

15 NOV 201

THE PAXMAN FEUD

Jim Branch was in sore need of a job. He'd been down on his luck the last few years and when young Wes Caufield hired him on to find out who was stealing his cattle he didn't say no—even though it meant he'd be little more than a hired gun.

Branch didn't know the job would put him dead center of a crossfire between the Paxman brothers—and that he'd have to stay there as a handy target to solve the mystery of the missing cattle. But between outgunning Vern Paxman and his toughs and out-thinking Floyd Paxman, Branch figured out how the celebrated Paxman feud had benefited none other than the Paxman brothers themselves.

THE PAXMAN FEUD

D. B. Newton

GUNSMOKE

First published in the UK by Chivers Press

This hardback edition 2007
by BBC Audiobooks Ltd
by arrangement with
Golden West Literary Agency

Copyright © 1967 by D.B. Newton.
All rights reserved.

ISBN 978 1 405 68148 3

All characters in this book are fictitious. Any resemblance to actual persons, living or dead, is purely coincidental.

British Library Cataloguing in Publication Data available.

LB OF REDBRIDGE LIBRARY SERVICES	
30108024724499	
Bertrams	08.11.07
	£9.95
REDKAC	

Printed and bound in Great Britain by
Antony Rowe Ltd., Chippenham, Wiltshire

THE PAXMAN FEUD

I

WHEN HE HEARD his station called—"Latigo, next stop"—Jim Branch unfolded cramped legs and rose, stretching to ease the kinks. Afterward, having swung a carpetbag down from the rack, he carried it through the daycoach, maneuvering the sway of the car in high-heeled and slightly runover boots. That carpetbag of his held a change of clothing and very little else, except for the Colt revolver wrapped in its shell belt and holster. His pockets were almost empty. Yet, despite his poverty, there was a pride to this man, which showed in the uncompromising set of his shoulders, and in the light-colored eyes that were almost startling against the weathered roughness of his face.

The face—like the worn boots, and the sweat-stained hat—marked him for a saddleman; by contrast his string tie and cheap town suit looked out of place, on a horsebacker's spare, loose-sprung body. Perhaps this was why curious eyes followed him, until the door at the forward end of the car swung shut at his back.

Out on the platform, between the cars, the wind held a strong spice of sage and sunwarmed pine. They were whistling for the station now, echoes beating back from the long, timbered ridge beyond the town that could be seen as a shimmer of sun-reflected roofs. Brakeshoes were beginning to grab and hold; Jim Branch set down his carpetbag and braced himself with a hand on the iron railing.

The first shacks slid past. There was an empty loading corral for cattle, and a switch—the railroad, he understood, was in process of building a spur north and west from here to tap undeveloped regions. Wheels rattled over rail ends; windows flashed the noon sun. The whistle sounded again and the bell began to clang. Down to a crawl, now, they eased up along the cindered apron fronting the mustard colored station. There the train halted, with a final grinding lurch.

Jim Branch gave no sign of being in a hurry to alight. While the engine hissed clouds of escaping steam he stood motionless, observing the activity that their arrival had set loose. Yonder, the stationmaster, in alpaca armbands and a billed cap, emerged from the depot toting a half-filled mail sack. A brakeman went by, tapping carriage wheels. Farther along, a freight car had already been opened and three men were at work unloading boxes and crates, while a clerk with a clipboard checked them off and another—a tall, cadaverously lean figure in a plug hat and a linen duster—gave orders, apparently bossing the job.

Now a man and a young woman came toward the coach platform where Branch stood. He looked at the girl; anyone would have. Dressed for traveling, she made a remarkably handsome picture with her pleasant features and masses of dark blonde, almost taffy-colored hair that was done up in a chignon under a pert little hat with a bird sewn on it. But at the moment she looked troubled. She was frowning, gnawing at a ripe underlip as she heard the earnest argument of the young fellow who carried her suitcase. At the foot of the iron steps she halted, shaking her head as she protested: "I still don't feel right about it, Wes. I just don't think this is any time for me to leave you!"

Jim Branch wouldn't need to have been told they were related. The young man—Wes—had the same color hair as she, the same good looks. He had on his work clothes—range garb, jeans and scuffed boots and a hickory shirt—and obviously he had come only to put his sister on the train. He had listened to what she had to say, but his mouth was firm as he told her, "Margie, we've had this all out before. Everything's been arranged. The McCabes are expecting you. You've more than earned a little trip—and you know you'll enjoy it."

"How can I enjoy it?" she exclaimed. "When I'll be wondering about you every minute, and if anything could be happening—"

"The only thing that's going to happen," Wes cut in, still patient, "is that this train will leave without you if we don't get you aboard."

He had her elbow and was guiding her firmly up the iron steps. The girl hesitated just once more— when she found herself face to face with Jim

Branch, and her eyes lifted to meet his briefly.

The effect on her was disconcerting. It was as though she read something in the stranger's face that startled her, something she didn't like; her full bosom lifted to a quickly caught breath. Branch looked over her head at Wes, who met his glance briefly before letting his own slide away. After that the two young people disappeared inside the coach, leaving Jim Branch with the memory of the girl's stare to trouble him.

It made a man wonder just how deeply the events of the past year or so had marked him—what brand there was in his eyes, that the barest meeting of looks could have had such a reaction on that pretty girl—a total stranger. It was enough to put a bleak edge to his thoughts as he got his carpetbag, and carried it on down the iron-treaded steps.

Solid ground underfoot felt odd, after twenty-four hours on the swaying daycoach. He walked over cinders, stepped up to the splintered wooden platform. A man went by him pushing a baggage truck and making the boards rumble. One leaf of the depot's double glass door stood open; Branch went in there and set down his carpetbag.

He looked around at the usual dingy scene—long, hard benches, a rusty stove set in a box of cinders, brass spittoons, a wall clock and a calendar and a blackboard for bulletins, with a piece of chalk fastened to it by a cotton string. There was no one at the ticket agent's window; but the station master came bustling through the room and Branch nailed him long enough for a question. "Can I make stage connections to a town called

Sharp's Creek?"

The man gave him an impatient answer. "That's in Holster Basin. Floyd Paxman, at the freight yard, has an old mud wagon he sends up there a couple times a week. If Friday ain't soon enough, you better think about hiring a rig."

Jim Branch frowned. "What about hotels?"

"Yeah, we got one of those. Right up the street —you couldn't miss it."

"Thanks," he said, and let the man go hustling about his business.

Returning to his carpetbag, Jim Branch stood just within the open door, watching the movement about the waiting train, as he took a cigar from the leather case in his coat pocket, and a kitchen match to light it with. He scratched the match along the doorframe and had bent to draw fire into the cigar when a pair of men, tramping past the door, stopped a moment within earshot.

One was saying, "—if you're real sure he's on there."

"Damn right I'm sure," the other answered. "I saw him get on—with the girl. We'll be ready to take him the minute he steps off the car."

"Suits me. You name the play...."

A voice shouted distantly, *"Board!"*

At once the speakers moved away; and Jim Branch was shaking out the match and tossing it aside as he thrust the cigar, still unlit, back into his coat pocket. He stepped out through the door into the full glare of sunlight beating off cinders and coach windows and iron rails. He was frowning, not liking what he had heard.

He saw the pair moving at a purposeful stride

toward the rear platform of the daycoach. They were a fine-looking set of toughs, in range clothing and sweated, shapeless Stetsons, each with a gun strapped to his leg. And now, past them, Branch saw the car door open and the young fellow—Wes —emerge and pause before he began to descend the iron steps.

It was as though a signal passed. Instantly one of the toughs broke into a sprint, pulling wide to gain the side of the daycoach where, at a crouch in the cinders, he brought up the gun from his holster. His partner had halted in the open, assuming a stance with scuffed cowhides placed well apart. The tail of his hand rested on a jutting gunhandle. The young man in the coach platform didn't seem aware of either of them yet. Plainly, the intention was to put him into a whipsaw, the instant he stepped to the ground.

Even if he was armed, he'd have little chance against a pair like this one.

Jim Branch remembered, too late, that his own Colt revolver was in the carpetbag, sitting inside the depot. No time now to get it. Instead he moved forward as the man in front of him raised his left arm and crooked a finger at the intended victim— an insulting gesture. His shout carried above all the other sounds about them.

"All right, Caufield. I'm waiting for you. Come ahead!"

Wes Caufield, holding to the grabiron, pulled his head around to stare; and Jim Branch waited no longer. His steady pace had brought him almost to the gunman. Lunging forward now, he covered the remaining distance and his reaching fingers descended on the man's shoulder.

At the last moment the other must have heard him; he whirled, sliding right out from under Branch's grab and nearly throwing him off balance as his hand closed on empty air. Quickly recovering, Jim Branch redistributed his weight with a cat-quick movement of his boots; then he was set and his right fist came scorching across the lifting face. He felt a scrape of wiry beard stubble, saw broad and ugly features that were distorted by surprise and by the shock of the blow. The man's head rocked back; his mouth flew open but nothing but a grunt of escaping breath came from it. Jim Branch caught a sour reek of booze.

Remembering there was still a second man, Branch knew he didn't have too much time. Deliberately he followed through his initial blow, left fist coming across in a short chop that made the darkbearded one's head roll helplessly like a punching bag. The heavy skullbone hurt his knuckles. He didn't hit again because he knew he didn't have to—he saw the result telegraphed in features suddenly gone slack, in eyes that rolled back in their sockets behind fluttering lids, in knees that lost their stiffening as the other started down. He fell heavily, like a disjointed doll.

At once a silent warning system was working, dropping Branch to his knees a fraction of a second before that gun over against the railway coach let go. He heard the smash of the shot, all but felt the passage of the bullet above his shoulder. The man he had knocked down was heavy, a solid weight of bone and muscle. Branch rolled him limply, got a hand on the Colt's wooden handle and brought it up in one swooping move.

When he fired he knew instinctively he had missed, and deliberately compensated for the action of a strange weapon by pulling slightly to the left for his second try. The sound of two guns mingled, bounced between railroad coach and depot front. Branch, still unharmed, saw his own bullet take the man yonder and slam him bodily against the side of the coach. His hat popped from his head, revealing a mop of fiery red hair; then he dropped, lifeless, into weeds and cinders.

Pandemonium broke loose all around Jim Branch. Men were yelling and running. At the train, faces of passengers filled the windows. And then the sound of someone coming up behind him brought him whirling to his feet and swinging the smoking gun.

Almost on top of him a man braked to a fast stop, as he saw the Colt's muzzle. It was the same one Branch had noticed earlier, bossing the unloading of freight from a boxcar. Now he had a better look at the cadaverously lean figure in linen duster and high wing collar, and plug hat set atop the wiry black hair. Branch suggested crisply, "You think you want in this?"

"No—no! Not me!" The man must have had a good deal more flesh on him at one time, for his cheeks and throat had sagging folds of flesh that wobbled to the violent shake of his head. He flung his hands wide to show they were empty.

Branch studied him intently. "All right," he grunted, not lowering the gun. "Then, you drift! I don't like you at my back!" His rough stare held, unyielding, until he saw the man hastily draw away; only then was he satisfied. He turned again to the tough he had felled with his fists.

This one was recovering; he had pushed up to hands and knees and was waggling his hanging head, as though to clear it. One big hand fumbled at his holster, found it empty. And Jim Branch suggested coldly, "Would this be what you're looking for?"

The man's head lifted; he stared blankly at the gun pointing at him. Then he seemed to recognize the weapon as his own, and memory rushed in on him and he bellowed hoarsely and surged to his feet; but the gun, and the look of the stranger holding it, halted him and made him keep his distance.

By now they were surrounded—train crew, station loiterers, passengers off the cars, all had come hurrying to the summons of the gunfire; departure of the train on schedule seemed a matter completely forgotten. A cluster formed about that other man lying in the cinders beside the tracks and quickly a cry went up that it was Red Shober, and that he was as dead as he would ever be— "The stranger plugged him square!" And they all looked at Jim Branch.

The harried stationmaster, black-billed cap askew, came elbowing through the circle that had formed at a respectful distance from the man with the gun. He pushed the cap back and stammered bewildered questions. He struck Branch as a man for whom such a break in routine was more than he could be expected to cope with.

"Just what the hell is going *on* here?"

"Don't look at me!" Jim Branch told him. "It was none of my mix. I never saw either of this pair before. I wouldn't have stepped in, except I realized they were setting it up to take that young fellow, there." He nodded toward Wes Caufield.

The unshaven tough, whose jaw showed the mark of the stranger's knuckles, let out a roar. "That's a damn lie!"

"*Is it?*"

This came from the intended victim. Up to now the young man had stood motionless, as though rooted to the steps of the daycoach by surprise and shock. Now, as he stepped forward, his face was drained of color but his voice was firm enough. "I think there's some in this crowd who knows what this is about, Nick Roddy! Though they're likely astonished as I am that it's actually come to murder!"

Nick Roddy glared at him. His hands were knotted into craggy fists and his lips pulled back in a mask of pure malevolence. He started to curse and broke off as he saw the dangerous glint that lit Branch's stare. In the crowd a voice said, "Somebody better get the law!"

"Deputy sheriff's out of town," someone answered; and another added sourly, "He *would* be, when he's needed!"

There was a sense of confusion and indecision. The stationmaster pulled off his cap, distractedly ran nervous fingers through his hair as he blinked behind steelrimmed glasses. "Damn it, *somebody* has got to take charge!" he exclaimed. "There's a man lying dead, yonder!"

Jim Branch looked at him. "Are you thinking of holding me for the law?" he demanded. "I'll tell you now—I shot in self-defense, and I shot second!

I wasn't even armed until I took this out of the big fellow's holster!" He showed the gun he was holding.

"He's telling the truth," a new voice unexptedly put in.

Surprisingly, it was the thin man with the predatory beak of a nose, the one who had startled Branch a moment ago by coming up too fast behind him. He had stood by, listening, and now he told the railroad man. "I saw the shooting, Frank. Red Shober began it; the stranger had no choice but to kill him. I'll tell that to the deputy sheriff, if necessary."

Branch hadn't expected this and he looked at the man in pure surprise. Nick Roddy, for his part, was driven to turn his savage anger on a new target. "Somebody's going to have to learn to keep their beak out of other people's affairs!" he snarled, and Branch saw the gaunt man's cheeks lose color; but he stood his ground.

The stationmaster mopped his forehead with a sleeve and pulled the cap back on again, saying hastily, "I can't see there's anything more *we* can do. Damn it, this train has got to roll! Somebody move that man's body...." He gave his orders. The engine's bell sounded again as, impatiently, the conductor and his crew started to herd their passengers back toward the cars. As casually as that the incident appeared to be closed; the crowd began to break and drift apart.

Jim Branch turned a cold eye on big Nick Roddy when the latter spoke. He had picked up his fallen hat, and now said roughly, "I'll take back that gun."

"You think so, do you?" Branch let him wait for it. First, he deliberately emptied it, spilling the shells upon the splintered boards of the platform. Rocking the cylinder home, he reversed the weapon and handed it over. "Shoots a little wide," he said calmly. "I'd have it worked on."

Roddy snatched the weapon and said in a voice that shook with dangerous feeling, "If you just got off that train, mister, you better get back on it. Because you might not like what happens if I catch you around here another time!"

"I expect to be around," Branch assured him. "You just be sure you know what you intend to do about it...."

A final glare, and the man holstered the empty gun and strode away from there, shouldering past someone who didn't get out of his way fast enough. Jim Branch watched him go, his eyes bleak. He didn't think that last, low-voiced exchange had reached any curious ears; but he knew that something had been set afoot, with his blow that laid Nick Roddy flat and his bullet that knocked the life from Red Shober, which was a long way from finished.

To a clanging of its bell and a huffing of steam, the train was rolling into motion. As he stood irresolute, there on the platform, three men went by him carrying Red Shober's lifeless body—the arms dangling, the head lolling limply, the shirtfront soaked with blood. Something in the sight of death tightened a clamp in Jim Branch's chest as he turned away, intending to seek a word with young Wes Caufield. The word went unspoken, for Caufield was occupied just then with someone else.

Instead, Jim Branch found himself staring straight into the face of the girl he judged to be the young fellow's sister.

Apparently she had made up her mind to let the train go without her, for her luggage was at her feet. It occurred to Branch that she had likely seen the fight, and the killing. Now she had watched the dead man being carried away. Jim Branch touched his hatbrim to her and said quietly, "I hope that's something that never comes so close again, ma'am." But then he broke off as he saw the look of fear and plain revulsion she gave him.

It made no difference, he thought bleakly, that in killing he had saved her brother's life. It was as though, in Jim Branch, she looked at some frightful species of animal.

He would not argue with that look. He had seen it before, and it never failed to wound; but somehow, on the face of this girl, it was especially hard to accept. His own mouth tightened. He nodded curtly, and turned and walked away.

II

AS THE STATIONMASTER had told him, the hotel was easy enough to recognize—a graceless hulk of a building, a story taller than most of its neighbors scattered along the street. Jim Branch carried his carpetbag there, impervious to the curious eyes of townspeople who, seemingly, all knew of the killing at the depot. In the musty-smelling lobby, that was separated by a pair of swinging doors from a barroom adjoining, he signed the register, got his key from the clerk and climbed creaking stairs to the second story.

He had been given a room at the front end of the hall; after dropping carpetbag and hat upon the sagging bed, he stood at the window for long minutes, looking thoughtfully over this town where he had received such a violent introduction.

It looked peaceable enough. From here the timbered hills tumbled away, with the dusty ribbon of stage road snaking northward—he supposed that would be the road to Holster Basin. As he looked he saw a freight wagon and team approaching along the road, trailing a feather of dust that the sunlight of late afternoon burnished to gold. They would be heading, he supposed, for the fenced-in wagon yard that he could see from his window, with the sign above the gateway that read: INTERMOUNTAIN FREIGHT—F. PAXMAN, PROP.

Turning from the window, he stripped out of his suitcoat and shirt and proceeded to wash away the grime of railroad travel, using the porcelain bowl and water pitcher on the washstand. He was working with the towel when a sound of knuckles at the door pulled him quickly in that direction. He tossed the towel aside, opened the carpetbag and dug out his sixgun, shaking it free of holster and shellbelt. With the weapon palmed and ready he said sharply, "All right! It's unlocked...."

The door opened. Jim Branch drew straighter, scowling a little, as Wes Caufield entered, ushering his sister ahead of him. With a grunt, he lowered the gun.

"Do you think you should have come here?" he demanded. "What if you were seen?"

"We were careful," young Caufield said. "The lobby was empty; I got your room number off the register. Anyway, what difference does it make now?" Still, he took a cautious glance into the hall before he closed the door. He said then, "This is my sister Margie."

Jim Branch nodded. Suddenly, under her solemn regard, he remembered he was partially undressed. Rather hastily he laid his gun on the washstand, caught up his shirt and slipped into it and worked at the buttons. The girl was dressed as he had seen her earlier—in her traveling suit, and the little hat with the bird. Her expression was still shocked and dazed and she seemed unaware that part of her fair hair had escaped from its coil on the back of her head. Branch told her, "Maybe you better have a seat. I'm afraid this, and the bed, is all I got."

He brought forward the room's single chair—stiffbacked, with a rung missing—and set it for her. After a moment's hesitation, and as yet without speaking a word, she took it.

She had not taken her eyes from the tall stranger's face, and their look still held a trace of the revulsion that had been in them earlier. Her brother explained, "I wouldn't have brought her along—but after what nearly happened down there, I think she's a little afraid to let me out of her sight!"

"You shouldn't either of you be in this room," Jim Branch said again. "If we're seen together, it ruins everything."

Wes Caufield stared. "You can't mean you intend going through with this thing?"

"I've come all the way from Ellensburg. You hired me to do a job. Are you firing me, before I've even started?"

"But—good Lord!" The young man spread rope-scarred and callused hands. "The risk! After that business on the station platform, you're a marked man at the very outset. To go ahead would be suicide!"

Branch shook his head. "I don't see it that way. These people have no reason to connect us. If it was openly known I'd been brought in as a range detective, the chances of my getting anything done wouldn't amount to much. This way—on my own, unhampered, simply a man and a gun on the make—I can play it by ear. As for my buying into your trouble with the pair at the depot—well, for all they have to know that was just one of those impulses. Nothing more."

"But Nick Roddy will be after your scalp, now. And Roddy is tough!"

"I can be tough, too," Branch replied shortly. "Isn't that what you're paying me for?"

The girl spoke then, for the first time; she had her emotions under control and her voice was calm as she looked at her brother, saying, "So, this has been planned between you, ever since you made that trip to Ellensburg last month. I suppose getting rid of me today—sending me away from the ranch and away from the Basin—that was all part of the plan, too!"

Patiently, Wes Caufield explained. "There has to be a showdown. It's coming, and it's sure. And if it means a fight—I don't want you in the middle of it. That's all I was thinking about when I arranged for you to visit the McCabes." He looked at Jim Branch, helplessly shaking his head. "Now she's made up her mind that she plain refuses to go!"

This was none of his quarrel and Branch merely shrugged; but something she must have thought she saw in his level stare roused the girl to anger. Her eyes flashing, she told her brother, "Maybe you've forgotten Seven Cross is my home, too, Wes Caufield! If there's to be a fight, I don't mean to leave it for—" She threw a scornful, flashing look

THE PAXMAN FEUD 19

at the tall stranger. "—for some hired gun, that we know nothing at all about. One who'd as likely as not sell us out to the other side!"

Her angry words stung the room's quiet for a moment. Jim Branch met the girl's stare; then his own expression closed down and, deliberately he turned to close the fastenings of his waistband. But when he took his hat from the bedpost, Wes Caufield finally realized what he was up to and cried sharply, "Wait, Jim! Don't go—she don't understand!" Seizing the girl by her shoulders, then, he made her face him as he said fiercely, "I'm going to tell you, once and for all, what I know about Jim Branch—things I was damned careful to learn, before I ever would have approached him with this job!"

"Let it go!" the other man said sharply.

But Wes Caufield was warmed to his subject. "Sure," he told his sister, in an angry voice, "you saw him kill Red Shober—only to save my life! Jim Branch is no common gunslinger for hire! He's a good man who's had some bad luck. The herd he was running, up in Montana, took the fever and wiped him out. To earn money for a fresh start, he took a job rodding the marshal's office in a Kansas cowtown, but he ran afoul of a crooked town council and because he wouldn't go along with the graft he was framed and thrown out of his job. That was a couple of years ago. Since then—"

Jim Branch had listened to enough. "I said, let it go!" he snapped, as he dropped his hat upon the bed. "My biography doesn't matter—and it doesn't change your problem. You told me at Ellensburg that your enemies were out to break you.

What I saw today, at the depot, indicates they're in a mood to go a lot farther than that!"

Young Caufield nodded tiredly. "It's never come to this before!" He had pulled off his hat; now he ran stubby fingers through his tawny mop of hair. "These past months, Vern Paxman seemed sure he could buy me out eventually—at his own price. And the longer I hold out, the more of my cattle are slaughtered and disappear. I've had fences torn out and line shacks burned; last week the springs at China Hat were dynamited and may never be usable again. And each time Paxman repeats his offer, the price is lower than the time before.

"But now, maybe he's finally run out of patience...."

"Maybe Nick Roddy was acting on his own?"

"Well—he's a killer," Caufield admitted. "And I think he was drunk. But I don't see him going against his boss' orders. Still, there's a lot about it I don't understand."

Jim Branch leaned his hips against the washstand as he considered. "Do you know why Paxman's so anxious to add your Seven Cross to his holdings in the Basin?"

"Not even that—unless he just wants it all. Ours is the only sizable spread left, among those he hasn't been able to take over since he came in two years ago. The rest are pretty small pickings. If we fall, he should gobble the others in short order."

Branch said, "One question that I didn't think to ask when we talked in Ellensburg, but it occurs to me now: What's the law doing, all this time?"

"The law," Caufield repeated, and shrugged. "I'd need some ironclad evidence that Paxman's

THE PAXMAN FEUD 21

behind my trouble, and so far I haven't got it. Meanwhile it's a long haul to the county seat, and there's not many votes in Holster Basin. Our sheriff finds it much more convenient to listen to whatever his deputy here in Latigo chooses to tell him."

"That would be the one who didn't show up this afternoon when he was needed?"

Wes nodded. "The same. Tell you the truth, I'm half convinced Lute Farmer is taking pay from Paxman to send his chief the kind of reports Paxman wants him to hear. I know *I* never been able to get any kind of satisfaction. When my crew started quitting on me, I decided it was time to bring in outside help. That's when I looked you up."

Branch was reminded of something that had been puzzling him. "Paxman: It's no ordinary name. Just who is this other one? The one who spoke up for me after that shooting at the depot? I understand he runs a freight line."

"Oh, yes. That's Floyd—he and Vern are brothers. But that doesn't mean he has anything to do with our problems. He came here independently, about a year after Vern, and started his freighting outfit; and he's been trying to use it to help build this country—not tear it apart. I have an idea he's actually ashamed of what Vern's up to, but he can't make an open issue of it; he's too frightened of Nick Roddy. For which I can't say I blame him."

"In that case, it must have taken nerve to stand up to him, the way he did today."

"Believe me, it took a hell of a lot of nerve! And Floyd would do more if he could. Just last week he called me in and offered to let me have a loan if it would be any use in weathering the storm, but of course I wouldn't take it. I can't drag him into an open fight with someone in his own family. It's bad enough that I've got *you* into this mess!"

Jim Branch let that pass. He thoughtfully rubbed the knuckle of a thumb across his cheek as he said, "The more I hear, the more certain I am the best way to break the thing open is to dive right into the middle of it. Maybe, if I'm lucky, I'll be able to turn up evidence against Vern Paxman that will make that sheriff go into action. It's always best to have the law on your side, if it can be managed."

Wes Caufield looked dubious. "Where will you start?"

"I don't know yet. I have to see how the hand is dealt. Right now, you folks better get back to your place, and give me a little time. I'll be getting in touch with you."

"All right, Jim." Caufield held out his hand. "I promised you a free rein, and I won't interfere now. Only—take care."

He turned to his sister, who had stood silent after her one brief outburst. Branch said quickly, "I'll check the hall," and he stepped to crack the door open and put a searching look both ways along the dingy corridor. All seemed clear.

Wes said, "We'll use the back stairs, to be safe." As Branch held the door for them, the girl hesitated and her eyes searched his face for a brief moment. He thought she had something she wanted to say; her lips seemed to tremble on an unspoken thought. But then, frowning, she averted her gaze and went past without a word. Her brother read Jim Branch's expression. He lingered for a brief word of explanation.

"I'm sorry. I apologize for Margie. You have to understand—she has good reason to hate the very idea of a hired gunslinger. You see, our pa was killed by one of them, when she was just a little kid. He was shot down right before her eyes!"

While Jim Branch digested that, the other man was gone. He stood and watched the pair move quickly and silently along the corridor, until they turned from sight at its end.

He turned back into the room, then, and slowly closed the door.

III

IN A THOUGHTFUL MOOD Jim Branch finished washing up, put on his string tie and then the cheap suit coat. From the carpetbag he got his shell belt and buckled it in place, settling the holster against his leg; checked the action and the loads of his Colt .45, and holstered it. With hat in hand he paused in the doorway to check the room before he stepped out into the hall and turned the key, afterward descending the stairs to the lower floor.

In the lobby, the desk clerk and another, who had the look of a gunhand, were engaged in conversation, but they fell silent and watched openly as he came down the steps. A third man, sprawled on the leather sofa, gave him a keen glance above the newspaper he held spread in front of him. Branch returned their looks, indifferently, and dropped his key on the desk where the clerk let it lie. Without breaking his deliberate stride, Jim

Branch crossed toward the adjoining barroom. His hand was raised to push open the swinging door when he heard the voice at his back: "You! Hold on a minute!"

Slowly he turned. The speaker was the one who had been talking with the clerk; he said, "Your name Branch?"

The stranger met his stare coldly. "You were just looking at it, there on the register."

"Reckon I was." The man came away from the desk a couple of steps, now. Behind it the clerk was blinking at Jim Branch with eyes that were dark holes in a face gone pasty white; his manner would have been enough warning that something was afoot here.

Over on the couch, the third man seemed lost behind his newspaper.

The one who had spoken was a nondescript type, with a sandy fall of moustache almost hiding his mouth, and eyes that seemed a little too close together. A rubberhandled gun rode the holster against his leg. The fingers of his right hand played a careless tattoo on the smooth leather of the holster as he said, in blunt challenge, "What's on your mind?"

Jim Branch, his eyes narrowing, answered as bluntly: "So far as it concerns you—not a single damn thing!"

"You're sure of that?"

"Very sure. Only thing that could interest me at the moment is a beer. A cold beer, with a pile of suds on top of it." Starting once more to shove the door open, he paused as the other slowly and deliberately shook his head. He said, in cold sarcasm,

"They do serve beer in there, I suppose?"

The other said, "They serve it better across the street. I'll show you."

"Not this time, thanks."

"Friend, that wasn't no invitation!"

The sudden iron in the man's voice brought him completely around, then. At the same moment there was the rattling noise of a newspaper being flung aside. In the hand of the man on the couch, a naked six-shooter tilted up in a point full on the tall stranger's chest.

Slowly, Jim Branch let his hand fall away from the swinging panel. He looked at the gun, at the face above it, and then again at the man with the sandy moustache whose hand rested now on the gun in his own holster. Behind the desk, the clerk was breathing heavily through a slack and gaping mouth.

Branch lifted his shoulders, in a shrug. "It begins to look like we go across the street...."

The man with the gun surged to his feet, and the two of them closed in on him. Remembering the incident at the depot, Jim Branch asked dryly, "Do you always hunt in pairs around here?" There was no answer. After that he was being marched out of the hotel lobby, leaving the clerk standing in back of his desk, pale and unmoving.

Evening was already coming on the mountains, a fan of afterglow spreading lemon-yellow above the western ridges and a window light or two showing here and there in the buildings of the town. There was almost no traffic on the streets at this hour. Face expressionless, and wasting no time on protests, Jim Branch let his captors direct him down the broad veranda steps, over the uneven sidewalk planks and at an angle across the strip of dust, which had been pounded fine as flour by the passage of hooves and wagon wheels. He saw at once that their goal was the big sprawl of a saloon, that appeared to be doing a fair amount of business. At least the hitch rail in front was lined with patient, saddled horses; as they angled past it to gain the sidewalk beyond, Jim Branch glanced at the brands and saw that a good many bore the Tomahawk brand belonging to Vern Paxman.

He was marched directly up the wide steps and in through the slotted doors, into a racket of voices and the mindless clatter of a mechanical piano working away at the nickel someone had fed into it.

The men scattered at the bar and at the tables were mostly ranch hands, together with a sprinkling of townsmen and even a trio in denim workclothes who shared a bottle at the bar; these last, Jim Branch decided, would be part of the railroad crew that he understood was laying track on the unfinished spur line, somewhere beyond the mountains. News of the stranger and of his exploits at the depot appeared to have reached here, too. The moment he entered, some of the talk died and a good deal of covert interest centered on him. He moved through it, looking neither to right nor left, his captors flanking him.

Nothing more was said about a beer, nor did Branch feel any great surprise at that. He was pointed directly toward a flight of stairs against the far end of the big room, which led up to a balcony and to what he supposed would be private gaming rooms opening off it. The three skirted a vacant dance floor and started up the steps, Jim Branch still offering no resistance but going along, instead, like a man who bides his time.

At the head of the stairs they turned along the balcony and halted beside a door where the one with the moustache laid his knuckles against the wood. A chair scraped floorboards; a muffled voice within demanded, "Who is it?"

"Me—Denver. We've got him."

The door was opened by a dumpy-looking individual in a sack coat that seemed to hang on him. A derby sat on the back of a mat of mousy, graying hair. Pinned to his waistcoat was a deputy sheriff's badge. Lusterless eyes peered at Jim Branch from behind deep pouches. Lute Farmer said, "So this is the one that done the shooting at the station.... All right, Teal. Bring him in."

As he moved out of the way for them to enter, Branch saw that the room's only other occupant was a man who sat reading a folded newspaper at the round cardtable that filled the center of it. There was a bottle and a couple of glasses on the table.

The deputy returned to a chair he had quit long enough to open the door, but the new arrivals remained standing. The one called Denver Teal heeled the door shut and then they all waited on the man with the newspaper. And he let them wait, while he took his time finishing an article that appeared to interest him.

Presently he dropped the folded paper onto the table and carelessly pushed it aside. Turning in his chair, then, he placed one elbow on the edge of the table and turned the weight of his slow scrutiny upon Jim Branch.

There was little seeming family resemblance between the two Paxman brothers, aside from their dark coloring and the piercing blackness of their stares. Where Floyd had been tall and gaunt, Vern Paxman was tall and heavy. The fingers he laced together across his middle were thick, callus-marked, and yellow with tobacco stain. But there was a sense of power about those hands, and about the chest and the solid set of the head upon his shoulders.

Prehensile, sensuous lips rolled the fuming stub of a cigar from one corner of the man's mouth to the other. Head on one side, Paxman studied the stranger. To Denver, the Tomahawk owner said in a rasping voice, "What's his name?"

Denver answered quickly. "Branch, the hotel register said. Jim Branch. I took this off him." He stepped forward and laid a .45 Colt revolver on the table in front of Paxman. The latter unlaced his fingers, picked up the gun and turned it over in his hands.

"It's just like any other gun," Branch told him shortly. "Except that it happens to be mine. I'd like it back."

Paxman pulled back the hammer, looked at the loads. He let the hammer off cock and placed the gun to one side. He took the whisky bottle, uncorked it, and poured a couple fingers of amber liquor into his glass. He had a thoughtful look.

"Branch," he repeated suddenly. "That has a familiar sound to it. You out of Kansas?"

"I've been there," he agreed, carefully.

"Yeah, I reckon you have! I guess you're the Jim Branch that killed the Texas Kid, in Hays City." Paxman nodded, his eyes narrowing, his heavy lips turning up in a half smile as though pleased at his own power of memory. But the smile quickly changed. The heavy jaw thrust forward and the stub of cigar wheeled. "And today you kill one of my hands, here on the station platform in Latigo! What's the big idea, Branch?"

The stranger lifted a shoulder. "Man shot at me. I shot back."

"You were mixing in something you shouldn't!" Paxman retorted, suddenly angry, leaning forward.

"That could very well be," Branch admitted blandly.

Paxman scowled. He plucked the cigar stub from his mouth, drained off the liquor he had poured, dropped the chewed butt into the empty glass. "I'm going to ask you a plain question, and I want an answer. Just what are you doing in this town?"

"At the moment, nothing," Branch said. "Except standing here listening to a lot of damn fool questions that I see no reason for answering!"

In the stillness of the room, someone behind him drew a sharp intake of breath. The lines deepened at the corner of Vern Paxman's mouth, and Branch found himself thinking, *I'm pushing too hard!* But if the big man showed irritation over these reckless answers, he sensed there was a growing respect in him too. Jim Branch decided he had read his man correctly.

Vern Paxman was probably not used to being treated so boldly. It was a good experience for him.

While he considered his next speech the rancher

reached into an inner coat pocket and brought out a cigar case made of silver. He opened it, selected one of the cigars. Afterward he started to put the case away again, then shrugged and offered it first to Branch. The latter grunted his thanks. The cigar even felt expensive; after the cheap brand he had been used to smoking, it was a real luxury. Paxman pocketed the case without including any of the others in his generosity. Branch sniffed the aroma of the weed with approval, bit the end off and followed his host's example by spitting it on the floor.

As he leaned to light up from the match Paxman held for him, he heard the door behind him open and someone entered the room. He resisted the nervous impulse to look around, calmly got the flame drawing the way he liked it. He stepped back and, then, as Paxman got his own cigar going, casually turned his head—and met the angry eyes of Nick Roddy.

It didn't take the furious stare of the tough he'd flattened on the depot platform to warn Jim Branch he was in maximum danger. These next few minutes were bound to be touch and go, and it took every ounce of nerve he possessed to meet Roddy's hating look with one of cool indifference while he calmly puffed at the cigar.

Paxman had seen the exchange of looks, observing it carefully. Now he shook out the match and dropped it into his whisky glass, and with a palm batted aside the cloud of smoke from before his face. "Branch, you don't seem the kind of gent that spooks easy," he said approvingly. "A man like that ain't too often come by. You wouldn't happen to be looking for work?"

"I haven't said otherwise," he admitted.

Vern Paxman liked that. "I can always use a good man. But he has to learn how to follow orders. Any man that can't, is no use to me at all."

Branch never got to make his answer to that. Nick Roddy had heard all he could take now and he broke in, fairly shouting: "Damn it, Vern! This is the bastard that killed Red Shober!"

The rancher nodded calmly. "I know. We were just discussing that."

"And you'd hire *him?*" Roddy pushed his way past the man called Denver, strode forward. "By God, you don't want a bastard like him on the payroll!"

Jim Branch turned his head and, across his shoulder, told the darkfaced man, "That's twice you've used that word, in as many sentences. One more time, friend, and I'll have to see about shoving it down your throat."

"Why, damn you—!" Branch expected the man to take a swing at him. Instead, even though he could see that the stranger was unarmed, Roddy obeyed a different impulse. He went for his gun.

Branch had no time to plan a counter-move. He saw the man's coat whip back, saw the arm rising and the blur of metal. He half turned, then pivoted back again. He caught that arm at wrist and elbow, the same way that, as a youngster in Montana, he had once grabbed a rattlesnake behind the head before it could sink its fangs in him. He cracked the arm across the point of his hip and Nick Roddy, with a hoarse cry, left the ground and took a flying spill that dropped him heavily upon his back.

He lost the gun—it struck the edge of the table

and went clattering against a wall. His hat fell off revealing a mop of coarse black hair with a bald spot on top. Then, Jim Branch, still retaining his grip on the wrist that had twisted Roddy's gun arm as the man spun floorward, took a step and placed one foot in the man's armpit and so held him totally helpless.

Sounds from the other men made him look around to see guns pointing at him from three directions, and danger in the scowling faces of those who held them. His jaw clamped on the cigar, which was still between his lips; he tightened his grip on that painfully rigid arm he was holding and said, around the cigar, "I can pull the arm clear out if you insist on it!"

Nick Roddy's face was wet with sudden sweat and twisted with agony. He shouted a protest to his friends, rocking his head from side to side in his anxiety, and the guns wavered. Then, still coolly unperturbed, Vern Paxman spoke from where he had sat unconcerned and unmoving during this brief burst of violence. "That's enough. Put away the guns. Branch, let him go."

The stranger waited until he saw the weapons holstered; then, with a shrug, he released the arm and stepped back. At once the man he had floored came rolling to his knees and crouched that way, nursing his sore arm and glaring at Branch through coarse, streaming hair. Nick Roddy said hoarsely, "For that, I'm gonna kill you! See if I don't!"

"Your privilege to try."

"And you ain't working for this outfit, either! You hear me, Paxman?" Roddy lunged to his feet, whirled to throw his ultimatum at his boss. "If he stays—I go! Take your pick. But when I quit, there's a good chunk of the crew will walk out with me. Including Red Shober's friends...."

Vern Paxman seemed to consider this, while he took another drag at his cigar and then carefully rubbed the ash from it against the rim of the shot glass. He shrugged, then, and lifted his eyes to Jim Branch. "Well, you see how it is. I can't have my crew unhappy; and Nick's one of my most valuable men. So under the circumstances, it looks like I'll have to withdraw the offer."

Branch hid his disappointment. He had gambled, and taken risks, only to lose the thing he had been playing for. In a tone he hoped sounded completely lacking in concern he said, "Just as well. I'm some particular who I work alongside."

The rancher went on as though he hadn't spoken. "Trouble is," he said calmly, "if you aren't going to work for me I don't think I much like the idea of you being around these parts. I suggest you think about moving on. Let's say, by tomorrow morning. At the latest." And his cold stare lifted to settle on Jim Branch, putting its weight behind the words.

The other's eyes narrowed and his jaw muscles hardened slightly. "I don't know; I only got here. I doubt I'll be in the mood to travel, by morning."

"The law might have something to say about that," Vern Paxman murmured thoughtfully. Without removing his stare he spoke to the deputy sheriff. "Lute?"

"Huh?" Oh, yeah—that's right." The man with the star jerked to attention, clearing his throat. Obediently, with an attempt at authority, he told the stranger, "You killed a man today, mister. From what I hear there's things about that shooting that could stand explaining. Sheriff may insist on it, if you happen to be around to remind me about mentioning the affair when I make my weekly report. I making myself clear?"

"Clear enough. I'll keep it in mind," Branch said; but he noticed how, for all his tough talk, the deputy's eyes shifted and wavered before his own steady regard. It told him all he needed to know about the caliber of the law in this Latigo country.

He looked back to the man at the table. "Well, I got a cigar out of it, anyway," he said. "Thanks for that. Now, if you'll hand me my gun . . ."

For just a moment, Paxman seemed to hesitate, while Nick Roddy seemed on the verge of violent protest. But the latter kept silent, scowling as he continued to rub his sore arm. And quite casually Paxman picked up the weapon from where it lay on the table beside him, and offered it butt-first. Branch took it and dropped it into the holster. He nodded, and turned on his heel.

No one in the room moved and no one spoke; only their eyes followed him as he walked to the door, opened it, and went out without another look behind him. He felt better when the door clicked shut.

IV

AT THE BAR downstairs, he stopped and had a drink while, on all sides, men viewed him with a covert interest. He ordered whisky, and he took it straight —by this time he needed something stronger than a beer to ease the tension across his shoulders, and put some stiffening in his knees, after that scene upstairs. There was also involved a deliberate challenge on his part, showing he had no intention of hunting cover.

Once he thought his challenge was about to be accepted; for glancing into the bar mirror, he saw Nick Roddy coming down the stairs, accompanied by the pair who had fetched Jim Branch from the hotel across the street. Immediately Roddy caught sight of his enemy, the mirror caught the run of dangerous feeling that broke across his angry face. But Denver Teal said something, shaking his head and placing a hand on Roddy's shoulder. The latter shook it off, in irritable gesture; still, he didn't argue. A moment later, having reached the foot of the steps, the three turned away into the crowd and Jim Branch was left alone.

Orders from Paxman, he supposed as he finished his drink—perhaps, a favor to the deputy sheriff who was plainly anxious to avoid any more open trouble. Whatever the reason, Branch was profoundly relieved.

Out on the sidewalk, he stood and smoked down his cigar and watched dusk settle over Latigo, while the spray of golden sunset faded above the hills yonder and turned them into a ragged cut-out shape. The evening star came out and a strengthening night breeze, weighted with the smell of pine and sage, breathed against him. It seemed to fan lamplight into brightness in the windows of the town.

So far, he thought bleakly, it looked as though he had completely bungled his job.

It had almost worked. Vern Paxman had seemed on the verge of taking him on until that wild man, Nick Roddy, laid down his ultimatum; now, for fear of tearing his crew apart and his authority over them, he plainly meant to have no part of the stranger. And so, by an unlucky run of chances, the scheme Branch had sold a reluctant Wes Caufield, as the likeliest way of getting to the bottom of things, had come to nothing. Not only that. With Nick Roddy out for his scalp and the local excuse for law ranged against him, he was inviting trouble with every moment he stayed around here.

It wasn't an encouraging situation. If Wes Caufield and his sister were not already started on their way home, the sensible thing would probably be to go look them up and admit he was licked.

But, damn it, he had taken too many defeats, of one kind or another, in these past few years! Failure could get to be a habit, and once he reached that point a man was doomed. Jim Branch had a feeling he was getting much too close to the end of the rope; to walk away from one more beating now could be a disaster—a real loss of nerve. It was a dim awareness, a glimmer of feeling, but it was no less troubling and it held him there in the growing dusk, pondering his bleak thoughts and a future that was like a wall or only a blackness, containing no hint of the way ahead.

He plucked the cigar from his mouth, flung it down and rubbed out the sparks with his bootsole, angrily. Across the way, lamplight picked out the letters painted on the plate glass of a cheap cafe, and this reminded him that a man must eat whether he felt any great appetite or not. There were still a few coins in his pocket, left after paying his railroad fare and an advance for his room. He settled the coat upon his shoulders and walked across the dark street, aware at every stride that Nick Roddy, and perhaps others of Red Shober's friends, might welcome a chance for a shot at him from the shadows. But a man couldn't hug safety forever.

As he approached the door of the eat shack, there was a scrape of boot leather near the building's corner. With a movement like a cat, Jim Branch leaped aside to put himself beyond the reach of light from the window; at the same instant he was palming his gun. He had it half way from the holster before a startled murmur reached him:

"My God, man! No!"

Hesitating, he demanded harshly, "Who is it? Mister, you better show yourself!"

"Not here," the voice insisted, holding to a whisper. "Branch, I want to talk to you. This is Floyd Paxman."

That was a surprise, but it left him no less cautious, filled with suspicion. "So you've learned my name?" he commented.

"Everybody in town knows it by this time." Branch could see the man's face now, dimly, a pale blotch in the dusk. Overhead the last steely light was draining out of the sky, giving way to a freckling of stars. A stillness lay on Latigo.

Floyd Paxman said earnestly, "What I've got in mind is a matter of importance—to me, at least, and I hope it may interest you as well."

"That's all right," Branch said indifferently, after a moment. "Only, just now I'm more interested in eating than talking."

"Sure. Go ahead. But afterwards—you know where my place is? The freight yard?"

"Yes."

"I have some work to do in the office. Come around when you're through; say, in a half hour. I'll be waiting."

Jim Branch shoved the gun back into its holster, smoothed down the skirt of his coat. All he would promise was, "I'll think it over," and with that he mounted the single plank step, pushed open the glassed door and entered the cafe, taking a sense of puzzlement with him.

After being turned down by one of the Paxman brothers, he couldn't help wondering what business the other one could have with him.

He had his meal—tough steak and lumpy potatoes and poor-tasting coffee, about what he was accustomed to from a thousand other meals in a hundred such cowtown grubshacks. He ate it at a pine counter that was spongy from countless scrubbings, giving his attention to his plate and ignoring the open stares of a half dozen other men. He was beginning to have a feeling that the town was interested in nothing else tonight.

Finished eating, he left his money on the counter beside his plate, got his hat off a wall hook and stepped outside, the eyes following him until the door closed. The town was tuning up a little as the night got older. A fiddle had joined the piano in the saloon across the street; shouts and occasional bursts of laughter drowned them both out. A big, white moon had risen, flooding the street with silver.

Jim Branch pulled his coat together against the chill off the high ridges, and turned in the direction of the freight line office.

Though he had made no promise, he had known curiosity would pull him this way. It stood on a corner lot, flush with the sidewalk, two wings of high board fence running off from it to enclose the freight yard. Through the archway of a wide gate he could see, by the lantern burning on a pole, the barns and sheds at the rear of the compound. There were parked wagons, and another vehicle he thought must be the mud wagon the railroad agent had mentioned.

Shades had been drawn at both door and front window, and somewhere within a lamp showed feebly. Passing under the tin awning he laid his knuckles against the door. He was about to knock again when he heard footsteps within. A voice said sharply, "Yes?" in a way that vaguely annoyed him. He identified himself and at once there was the sound of the lock turning and the door swung part way open.

"You're sooner than I expected," Floyd Paxman grunted. "Come in—come in." He stood aside for his visitor, then quickly shut the door and the latch clicked. "Come on back here," Paxman said. "Have a seat."

There was nothing elegant about this office, built as it was of plain pine lumber and furnished haphazardly. Branch saw a bookkeeper's desk with a tall stool in front of it, a bank of filing cabinets, a few straight chairs. Beyond a low railing, an oil lamp burned above a desk that was laden with papers and ledgers. Definitely apparent was a strong odor of horses and dung drifting in from the stable in the yard just outside.

Apparent, too, he thought, was the smell of fear from this man who hid in the shadows, and sat alone in his office with the door locked and the shades pulled to the sill. . . .

Jim Branch followed the other through a gate in the railing and took the chair that was offered him. Floyd Paxman dropped into his swivel chair and with a sweep of an arm pushed a space clear amid the litter on the desk between them. Studying him in the streaky yellow lamplight, Branch could again see only a faint resemblance to the big man in the card room of the saloon. Unlike his brother, who had a neat air of masterful competence, Floyd

Paxman was as untidy as his work habits. The high collar and string tie clung askew to his scrawny neck. The bushy hair stood up as though he must run his hands through it constantly; and though he had shaved, he had done a careless job—a few wiry spikes of beard still bristled high along his cheekbones.

There was to be no offer of a cigar from this member of the Paxman family. Floyd settled back, lacing bony hands in front of his waistcoat; his thumbs fiddled nervously with an elktooth charm dangling from the chain that looped there, while he stared fixedly at his visitor. After a moment Jim Branch found this vaguely irritating. He crossed his legs, hung his hat on one boot toe, and said gruffly, "Well, this was your idea, Paxman. What's on your mind?"

"To be brief," the other said, "I was thinking you might be looking for a job."

"What makes you think I haven't already found one?"

The black eyes narrowed; Floyd Paxman didn't like that answer. "Surely not with my brother? Not after what happened at the depot!" When Jim Branch merely looked back at him, not replying, the freighter moved his shoulders in an angry gesture. "At least give me a chance," he snapped. "Tell me what he's offered you. I'll raise it a hundred."

"For quitting him? And coming to you instead?" Branch tilted a quizzical look at the man. "Is it really worth all that, just to keep me off his payroll?"

"That," Floyd Paxman said curtly, "is my business. All I want from you is a yes or no!"

Branch took his hat from his boot toe and spun it between his hands. "Let's start over again," he said at last. "The fact is, I'm *not* working for your brother. So if I like your proposition, you can forget the extra hundred."

The gaunt face actually broke into a smile. "You're an honest man, at least. We should get along." Leaning forward, Paxman opened a desk drawer and set out a bottle, following it with a couple of glasses. "Join me?"

"Why not?"

The freighter popped the cork with his thumb and filled both glasses, reached across to hand one to Branch. He saluted his guest with his own glass and emptied it, smacked his lips.

It was good, smooth whisky. Branch nursed his along. Two drinks in a single evening was his limit, and he'd already had one just before supper. He looked at the amber jewel, which the lamplight found in the glass in his hand; he said, "Suppose you tell me what makes you think I'm the one you want, for whatever you've got in mind...."

"I liked the way you handled yourself in that business at the depot. It showed courage, and quick thinking. And it turns out I've heard of you. A town tamer, I understand. You're supposed to have done something of a job over in Kansas."

"I tried," Branch said with a shrug. "Why? You got a town that wants taming?"

"It's not exactly my town," Floyd Paxman said; "though, I've invested a stake in it and I'm concerned for its future. And it doesn't need to be tamed. It's really a nice little town, in fact. I just want to keep it that way!"

"What town would we be talking about?"

"It's a place a little north of here. Called Sharp's Creek."

Jim Branch was looking into the half-filled glass, and so his eyes failed to betray his sudden flash of interest. Paxman continued: "With the railroad building so close I see a good future for all that country, if it's only allowed to develop. I'm running freight and stage service into Holster Basin now, and I own a store and other businesses there. What's mostly needed is more people. And I think there'd be a good chance of getting them—if it wasn't for one man."

"Let me guess," Jim Branch murmured. "Your brother . . . ?"

Floyd Paxman shot him a look. "What have you heard? That he owns half of Holster Basin and is after the rest? Maybe you even heard that the young fellow you stopped Nick Roddy from murdering, this afternoon, is the main thing standing in his way?"

"You don't seem to approve of your brother Vern. . . ."

"We're at swords' points!" Floyd snapped. "It's reached the place where he's threatened bringing his crew into Sharp's Creek and burning it—tear the town down around my ears. Now, that was just a bluff, of course. Still—"

"You want insurance," Jim Branch finished. "You want a gun of your own up there to see that it doesn't happen. . . . All right." He polished off his whisky, set the empty glass on the desk. "When do I start?"

Floyd Paxman blinked. "You'll take the job?"

"I've had no better offers."

"Well, fine! Fine! Another drink—to seal the bargain?" In sudden good spirits, the freighter picked up the bottle but Branch covered the glass with the palm of his hand, shaking his head. Paxman poured his own drink, tossed it off. He said, "I've got a load of freight moving up to Holster, tomorrow morning. Why don't you ride the wagon? Take a look around; get the lay of the town; meet the people there. I expect to be coming up the day after, at which time I'll likely have some further instructions for you. How does this sound?"

"Good enough." Jim Branch got to his feet. "One little thing. I'll want a month's pay—in advance."

He made his demand coolly enough, chiefly curious to see if he would get it. Plainly, the other man was somewhat less pleased about this detail; a shadow of a scowl passed over his face but was as quickly gone. He shrugged, and, pulling open a drawer of the desk, took out a tin strongbox. He opened it, and Branch saw a flash of green bills and silver and gold pieces. He waited as Paxman counted out a small sheaf of bills, tossed them onto the desk, and closed the box. "Will that do?"

He picked up the money, ran a corner of the greenbacks across his thumb and negligently thrust them in his nearly empty pocket. As he did so a faint sourness tinged his thoughts; he found himself wondering suddenly. *Then am I really becoming a gunman for hire?* And the image of Margie Caufield's pretty and disapproving eyes rose to trouble him.

He dismissed the thought, angrily. He had nothing to be ashamed of. He'd wanted a way to get to Holster Basin, hadn't he—any way that would disguise his connection with the Caufields? Since he had failed his initial hope of signing on with Vern Paxman's crew, hiring himself out to the other Paxman brother would serve the same end. And if Floyd and the Caufields were both bucking Vern Paxman, then the chances were even good that he would actually earn this advance stake he'd wangled. He would go to Sharp's Creek and see where the trail led from there.

"In the morning," he said, and pulled on his hat. Floyd Paxman walked him to the door. As it closed behind him he heard the key turn quickly in the lock.

V

MORNING FRESHNESS was in the air, the shadows in the street lying long and sharp-edged, when Jim Branch left the hotel and walked across the dust to the freight yard carrying his carpetbag. Early as it was he found a canvas-topped wagon loaded and its mule team standing in harness—and Floyd Paxman's driver fumingly impatient. "You're my passenger, I reckon," he said sourly as Branch came under the high archway of the gate. "Where the hell you been? I been ready and looking for you, this past fifteen minutes."

"Sorry. I didn't know. Paxman never mentioned a time."

The muleskinner shrugged aside the apology. "Throw your gear in back and climb aboard," he ordered grumpily. "We're burnin' daylight. . . ."

His name was Hamp Billis—a reedy, sunburnt man in his middle fifties, below average height but with shoulders and arm muscles so developed from years of handling his animals that he looked nearly deformed. It might have been long association with mules that made him cross-grained and ill-tempered; at least, Branch soon decided it was useless trying to get any civil communication out of him. He tried to learn how long Billis had been working for Paxman and got no more than a grunt in answer. He gave it up then, resigning himself to a dull and unsociable trip.

They rolled north, leaving the town of Latigo and the molten streak of silver that was the railroad; the road they followed—scarcely more than twin ruts, which the passage of heavy freight rigs like this one had carved deep in the sandy earth—skirted the high, timbered ridge at their left, threading through sage and occasional stands of pine. This was cattle country, though occasionally one could still see the scars of mining operations that had either played out or never actually come to anything.

Ahead, more hills were building up and presently the ground began to break and lift as they climbed. Branch ventured to ask his silent companion, "How far to Holster Basin?"

"Twenty miles, from the rails." Hamp Billis nodded to the rises ahead, blue with distance. "We cross them there hills by Rabbit Ear Pass."

"Pretty good country, up in there? Rich grazing?"

Billis hunched his misshapen shoulders. "Ask somebody else," he grunted. "All I know's mules. That's enough headaches."

One thought had occurred to Branch, and he offered it now. "Looks to me the railroads are taking the country over. The spur line that's building up this way, just to the west of the hills—I suppose that will eventually tap Holster. I'd say, eventually, people like you and your boss will be out of business."

The other shrugged again. "Rails can't go everywhere." If he was worried about the future of his livelihood, it would have been hard to sort this worry from his general surliness.

Still the earth crumpled under them, lifting them higher, leaving the dun-and-green stretches of the rangeland below. They rode through thick timber where the smell of the pines, drawn out by midmorning sun, swam thick and sweet about them. The trees fell back and now the road shaped up as a zigzag pattern of switchbacks, climbing a bare brown face of rock where only scrub growth could cling. Jim Branch clung to his place and put his trust in the wagon, the mules, and Hamp Billis' skill in handling both. The steep turns, the sheer climbs, where the turning wheel hub on his side of the wagon alternately threatened to scrape the cliff or hung suspended over empty space, were unsettling to a man who was more familiar with the flat stretches of western Kansas prairie.

This was plainly old stuff to Billis, however; and the mules proceeded with their unperturbed and earwagging calm. They reached the top of the grade presently and here the team halted, apparently of their own accord. Billis, kicking at the brake bar, announced shortly, "I let 'em rest here. Might stretch your legs."

A seep spring, making a flashing run over sun-heated granite, fed a grassy pocket of meadow. Billis unhitched his mules and led them by pairs down to drink and graze, while Jim Branch walked about finishing one of the cigars he had bought that morning out of his advance wages. The air was bracing, cool despite the sun and just thin enough, at this altitude, that a man reached to fill his lungs when he breathed. The hills stretched away in folds of green trees and shining granite. A hawk swung on motionless wings, high under the deep blue dome of the sky.

Jim Branch had not been hired to work mules and he didn't volunteer his help now, figuring the cross-grained skinner would probably want no one else messing around with them. The feeding and watering accomplished, Billis was returning them to the wagon, hooking them into the harness again. Done with his smoke, Branch tossed the butt away and turned to resume his place on the seat, but he saw that the other wasn't ready yet to go. The man was checking harness, minutely studying a length of leather hame and taking his time about it. Branch waited. The minutes passed.

The harness having apparently stood inspection, Hamp Billis walked around the wagon, looking at the wheels, going down on his ankles to peer underneath at the underrigging. Only as he remembered the man's surly haste earlier that morning, did Branch begin to wonder at the time he was wasting now. He saw that Billis' narrow, darting glance was busy, squinting at the sky and at the surrounding rocks while he pretended to be studying the rig. It was this that caused suspicion to form and harden in him.

His jaw set. "Maybe you've got all day," he said sharply, "but I'd like to get where I'm headed. Let's be going!"

That brought Hamp Billis to his feet, jerking angrily about. "Who's giving who orders?" the man started to say belligerently. But he looked into the taller man's face and something he saw there appeared to take the arrogance out of him. He hesitated; he ran his tongue around inside his mouth. His shoulders fell, then, and his eyes slid away from Branch's. "I was just fixing to get started," he muttered. "Climb on."

He went shuffling around to the other side of the wagon, and hoisted himself up to the seat. Still wondering about his odd behavior, Jim Branch walked over, set his boot on the hub of the big wheel and swung up. He was about to step into the wagon's box when a rifle bullet suddenly struck the hickory bow beside his head, and then the splat of the rifle itself reached his ears.

A voice called sharply: "Hold it, Branch! One move and you're dead!"

His head jerked. Sitting his horse, motionless in a saddle of rock between two tall boulders, a rider was silhouetted with a smoking carbine in his hands. He cranked a fresh shell into the breech, sunlight making a smearing arc of the empty as it spun clear; now the smoking muzzle was lined up and ready for a second shot. The man was Nick Roddy.

Caught in an awkward position, perched on the edge of the wagon box, Branch could not have made any kind of move. He stayed frozen as he was; and now two more riders came into sight, moving through the gap on either side of Roddy and spurring down on the wagon without coming between that carbine and its prey. One of these was the man called Denver Teal—he of the flowing, sandy moustache who had taken Branch across the street from the hotel to see Vern Paxman, last evening. The other was one he didn't recognize, but he didn't doubt it was one of Paxman's crew.

They circled and came up on two sides of the wagon, and as they pulled in and steadied their horses each had a sixshooter in his hand. It was Denver Teal who lifted the gun from Jim Branch's holster and dropped it into a pocket of his coat. "Now," he said gruffly. "Step down."

Branch dropped lightly to the ground, his face expressionless, his eyes carefully watchful. Now Denver turned to Hamp Billis, who sat hunched on the seat holding the reins. "Git!" he ordered.

Billis said not a word. Jim Branch had noticed the shine of a twin-tubed shotgun under the seat of the wagon, but the muleskinner made no attempt to reach it, nor did the captors bother to take it from him. They merely pulled their horses aside, out of the way, while Billis kicked off the brake and yelled his mules into motion.

The long ears pricked forward and the teams responded. The heavy wagon lurched away, picking up momentum as it rolled onto a slight downhill grade. Boulders and trees swallowed it; a curtain of dust settled and gradually the sound of hooves and chains, of straining timbers and rumbling wheels was blotted into silence.

Jim Branch looked around as Nick Roddy came spurring down out of that rocky saddle. The carbine was in its scabbard now and he was leading a saddled horse. His heavy, brutish face still bore the marks of Jim Branch's fists, but it also wore a look of savage pleasure. His lips peeled back; white teeth showed in a grin.

Grit spattered Jim Branch's legs as Roddy pulled in, dropping the leathers of the lead horse. Deliberately the man swung down, letting his own chestnut gelding's split reins fall to ground-anchor it. As he stood facing the man who had twice beaten him, the anticipation of pleasure deepened on his face; he dropped his head forward a little and his hands balled into fists.

Denver Teal, from somewhere in back of Branch, spoke up a little uneasily. "What are you gonna do to him, Nick? You know, Vern said—"

"I know what he said," the big fellow answered gruffly. "If he wants him he can have him. But he'll wait till I'm through!" And suddenly, as though something had tripped a spring inside him, he lunged at this man he hated.

Even with guns covering him, Branch meant to defend himself. He had been poised for the charge and he faded away from it, his own right fist coming over. His knuckles bounced off the same flat cheek he had bruised in the fight at the depot, and he heard Roddy's grunt of pain and anger. Roddy's own, confident blow had failed to land at all. He shook his head, roaring, and went after Branch, and the latter dropped back again.

But now his shoulder struck an obstruction—the flank of Denver Teal's horse. When he tried to sidestep into the clear, an arm came suddenly down from above him; it encircled his throat and lifted.

He was pinned there against Denver's leg, with the crook of Denver's elbow tightening under his chin and yanking his head up to hold it helpless as in a vise. And then Nick Roddy was on him.

He couldn't move; he could not do anything. Roddy's huge fist came squarely toward his face, seeming to blot out the sun. He tried to turn his head, in vain. He felt his mouth smashed under the direct blow, felt the blood spurt hotly. He heard Roddy's laugh and saw the arm draw back for a second driving blow at a helpless target.

In desperation Jim Branch bent his knees, let all his dead weight fall limp against the crook of Denver's arm. He thought he was going to strangle; blackness pulsed behind his eyes with the beat of his own heart. But his weight threw too great a burden on Denver and just as Nick Roddy hit a second time, the grip broke around Branch's throat and he slipped free. Roddy's smash took him glancingly on the forehead and knocked the hat from his head; he slid down Denver's leg and into the weeds at the feet of Denver's horse. Gasping for breath, he rolled and scrambled under the animal, which was stepping around frantically while its rider cursed it. One hoof struck his arm and numbed it clear to the shoulder. Then he was trying to roll free as Nick Roddy, bellowing in fury, slapped the horse on the rump to get it out of his way so he could come at his enemy.

On his knees now, Jim Branch looked up and saw that Roddy had pulled a gun. The muzzle loomed blackly at a level with his eyes; he could only stare at it, and at the splayed thumb which pulled the hammer back. Still dazed by the blows he had absorbed, he knew there was not a thing he could do to stop the bullet that, in another moment, would blow his brains out.

Then, from his saddle, Denver Teal exclaimed harshly, "Nick, cut it out! This ain't what Vern wants!"

"It's what *I* want!" the blackheaded man said; but with an angry shrug of meaty shoulders he let the hammer down and lowered the gun. Thwarted rage made him ugly. "All right, bucko," he told Branch, scowling. "We'll give Vern his chance at you. Mine comes later." He lifted his head, sought out the third rider. "Crane, bring that other bronc over here...."

Crane was a loose-coupled man with a lantern jaw and a slight cast in one eye. He caught up the reins of the horse Nick Roddy had led in and came up with it, and Roddy waggled his gun at Branch and ordered briefly, "Get on him." Branch looked at the reins that Crane held out to him. He touched a sleeve to his lip that was swelling where Roddy's fist had smashed it; he gathered a mouthful of saliva and blood and spat it into the dirt. Then, without a word, he took the leathers and hauled himself onto the back of the animal—a roan gelding.

One thing he knew for certain: It had been no accident that they brought an extra saddled mount with them....

Nick Roddy pouched his gun, went to get his own horse. While they waited, Jim Branch looked at Denver Teal. "You kept him from using a bullet on me," he said. "I have to thank you for that."

The man with the sandy moustache merely gave

him a look and a shrug. "Don't bother," he grunted. "You've looked like trouble to me from the start. But Vern Paxman pays my wages and I try to give him what he wants. Otherwise, Nick could blow your head off, for all I care."

"Thanks," Jim Branch said dryly as Roddy came up, mounted and ready to go. "I'll remember you said that. I wouldn't want you to do me any favors. . . ."

VI

THEY LEFT THE wagon ruts behind them and struck out across unmarked country, following a route known only to Jim Branch's captors, dropping once in a while into an occasional stock trail. The trend was north, and though they stuck to the high country he judged they were still headed in the general direction of Holster Basin.

Overhead, the sun swung over as the day grew older, and creamy thunderheads began to pile up behind the timbered granite ridges; one of those quick mountain storms seemed in the offing. Presently, a blatting of cattle sounded. Nick Roddy pulled rein and now a jag of steers came moving up toward them through a sparsely timbered draw—a dozen head or so, with three riders pushing them. These came on warily until Roddy lifted a hand and called greeting; as soon as they recognized him their caution fell away and they seemed to forget the guns in their holsters.

The horses, like the ones Branch and his captors rode, had Tomahawk brands. But the cattle all bore Caufield's Seven Cross.

Nick Roddy, with a squint at the threatening sky, said pleasantly, "Looks like we could all get wet, don't it?"

The leader of the three ignored the comment. A yellow-haired tough with a droop to one eyelid, he was looking narrowly at the stranger. "New man?"

"Hardly! He's a fellow that give us some trouble at Latigo, yesterday. The bastard done for Red Shober, believe it or not! Vern said for us to pick him up, soon as he left town."

The man's eyelid drooped lower. He hadn't missed Branch's curious inspection of the cattle with the Caufield brand. He said suspiciously, "Getting himself quite an eyeful, ain't he?"

"Hell of a lot of good it will do him!" Roddy grunted. Jim Branch heard the threat behind the words but it hardly affected him. He already knew he was not meant to survive this capture very long.

After a further brief exchange that told him nothing, they rode on leaving the obviously stolen cattle and their handlers. The clouds moved across the sky and the wind turned chill, but the threatened rain held off. Jim Branch made no attempt at conversation and asked no questions, because he knew his captors would tell him only what they wanted him to know.

He was sure now they must be in the hills above Holster Basin, in a country that was likely used as summer range; the signs of stock movement were plain, and once or twice the trail they were following brought them out onto a point that gave him view of lower hills and a glimpse of cloud-dulled rangeland far below.

He mapped the country as best he could, trying to memorize what he could see as they traveled through it. It was obvious that they weren't taking him directly to Tomahawk headquarters; he learned what their real goal was when they broke at last out of a fringe of pines and he saw a log shack —a line cabin, apparently—sitting at the edge of a tight pocket of meadow.

Grass brushed their stirrups as they rode up to the door and halted. Nick Roddy got down, untwisted a piece of wire that held the door shut in lieu of a padlock, and walked in. After a moment he was back, to tell Denver Teal, "Bring him in. There's grub enough for a few days, blankets on the bunks if you need them. It will do to hold him until Vern decides what he wants."

Branch had thought for a moment they meant to lock him up and leave him here alone, but it appeared that Teal was being given the job of guarding him. He was ordered from the saddle, and while Crane led his and Denver's horses away to the nearby pole corral to unsaddle them, Branch was marched inside.

There were the furnishings one would expect—a crude deal table and chairs, a squat-bellied stove, a wall cupboard holding foodstuffs. A tier of bunks was against one wall. The cabin held the chill of a place long closed up and unused. Nick Roddy told Denver Teal, "No one's apt to bother you. If anyone does show up, I'm leaving it to you to make sure they don't see our friend."

"They won't," Denver promised. "But I hope I ain't stuck here long, with a storm coming. I never did play jailer before!"

Roddy shrugged and looked darkly at the prisoner. "Don't take nothing off the bastard. If he acts funny, plug him."

A moment later he was gone, shutting the door after him; the sound of horses faded as he and Crane rode away. Branch was left alone with his guard.

The latter had drawn his gun. He took a seat at the table, placed both elbows on the wood and laid the weapon in front of him. He said, "Let's see you make yourself useful. Light us a fire and warm up this damn place. And don't try anything while you're about it."

Without a word, Branch turned to the chore. There was kindling, a pile of pine chunks in a box beside the stove. Laying the fire, he weighed a chunk of wood in his palm and, for just a moment, measured its potential as a weapon; but a glance at Denver and the gun lying in front of him was enough to show the futility of that. Before he could make any move he would be a dead man. He pushed the thought aside, and proceeded with his chore.

Soon a blaze was crackling in the stove, roaring in the chimney which began to pop as the cold metal expanded. Branch set the damper, once the fire was going well, and the warmth of it began to spread and drive the chill into the corners. He wiped his hands on his pants and looked to Denver for further orders.

"Might as well take the load off your feet," the

man said, not unpleasantly. "No telling how much time we got ahead of us. Ain't that a pack of cards on the shelf?"

They were cards, battered and dog-eared and so coated with grease and dirt that a man would almost have to wet a thumb and scrub their faces in order to see the pips. Branch didn't feel much like games but there was little else to do. He took a seat opposite Denver while the latter took the deck and began to shuffle.

Suddenly the man paused, gave a sharp look at Branch and at the gun lying between them, in too easy reach of the prisoner's hand. The sandy moustache lifted in a humorless grin, showing white teeth; Denver picked up the gun and slipped it into his holster where there could be no danger of the other man getting ahold of it. "Blackjack all right?" he suggested pleasantly, when that was taken care of.

Jim Branch shrugged. "One game's as good as another."

They played desultorily, no money changing hands, merely killing the dragging hours. As the warmth of the stove spread through the cabin, Denver Teal unbuttoned his coat and, presently, rose to shuck out of it and lay it on the top bunk of the tier in the corner. Branch, shuffling the cards, paused as he saw that and his eyes narrowed for a moment; then he resumed his mechanical motions, anxious not to betray any hint of his thoughts.

The game continued in halfhearted fashion, neither man really interested. A murky, filtered glow of sunset poured in through the cabin's single window, and after that dusk quickly began to fill the room. Denver yawned and scratched his ribs; he said, "The hell with this. I'd have thought there'd been some word, by this time. Me, I'm getting hungry." He left his prisoner to collect the cards while he himself rose and got the shack's one oil lamp to burning. He added wood to the fire, and then began to search the shelves.

Still, he was nonetheless alert to any move Jim Branch made. When he heard the latter's chair scrape back he turned quickly, a hand moving cautiously to the gun in his holster. Branch merely yawned and placed his hands against the small of his back as he stretched. Still keeping a wary eye on him, Teal dug up a clasp knife and used it to saw open the lid of a can of beans he had located. Jim Branch walked over to the tier of bunks, where he had flung his own coat and hat beside Teal's.

He picked up his coat, dug into a pocket and got out his leather cigar case, which fortunately had survived, undamaged, the fight with Nick Roddy. He took out a cigar, bit off the end, returned the case. From his shirt pocket he dug out a match, prepared to scratch it alight on the wooden frame of the bunk.

Denver Teal had turned to place his beans on the stove to heat, and for that moment his suspicions and his watchfulness were eased. Branch, seeing this, recognized the chance he had been waiting for. He dropped both match and cigar as he made a quick dive for Teal's coat.

Through the cloth he could feel the hard shape of his sixgun which, he judged and hoped, the other man had forgotten; but unluckily he had to flip the garment over in order to find the pocket opening. As he did, the flap of the pocket got in the way of his fingers. He fumbled at it, groped and he felt cold metal under his hand.

Yonder at the stove he heard the can of beans tumble to the floor as Denver's sleeve knocked it from the stove. When he turned, at last ripping the gun free, he saw the other man just pulling his own weapon from the holster. Branch could have shot him, but something stayed his hand. After all, this was the man who, by speaking up, had prevented Nick Roddy from murdering him. And so he held off the trigger, for that one fateful moment, instead saying sharply, "Teal! Don't do it!"

It was a mistake—almost, his last one. That other gun blurred upward faster than he would have thought possible; obviously, Denver Teal was a real gunman. In a killer's crouch he drew and tilted the muzzle of his gun and fired, and a lance of fire struck Jim Branch with a blow that drove him back, hard, against the frame of the double bunk. The Colt flew from his hand, struck the puncheon floor and lay spinning.

He had followed it with his eyes and, despite the numbing pain in his bludgeoned left arm, made a desperate move to go after the sixshooter. He was bending to scoop it up when, with a rush, the shape of Denver Teal came at him. He twisted his head around, saw the gleam of a gunbarrel descending. He tried to move aside, and the blow that was aimed at his skull struck across the back of his neck and glanced off the shoulder of the wounded left arm.

He dropped, senseless.

He awoke, laying belly down, with his face pressed into the folds of smelly, musty blankets. When he attempted to move he could do no more at first than roll his head slightly, so that he could at least gulp cleaner air into his lungs. The glow of the oil lamp struck his eyes. He was lying on the lower bunk in the line cabin; he had a feeling that an hour or two might have passed.

After a moment he tried again to turn over and found his limbs trapped and powerless. Raising his head with an effort, he saw now the ropes that tied his wrists to the bunk timbers; he judged his ankles must be anchored in the same way and that he lay spreadeagled, helpless. He saw too the blood soaked into his left sleeve and into the blanket, from where a bullet had scored his left shoulder. The whole arm ached with a dull throb; his skull was racked by a pulsing agony from that blow with the gunbarrel. He dropped his head again, gasping, and waiting for greater strength to build up in him.

That was when he became aware of the voices. They were not in the room with him; he realized instead that the door had been left open, letting night chill seep into the stuffy heat of the roaring stove, and that two men were just outside. He heard Denver Teal's voice: "—sure as the devil suits me. Riding herd on this guy ain't any picnic. He's a mean bastard! He actually tried to get a gun; I had to shoot him up a little."

A voice that sounded like the man named Crane said, "Well, Vern wants to see him. Tonight."

"All right," Teal grunted. "Saddle the horses while I get him on his feet. Let's move out of here in a hurry. That rain ain't going to hold off much longer...."

As Crane's steps moved away in the direction of the corral, Denver Teal came inside, and closed the door. Branch remained as he was, motionless and with eyes closed. Teal's shadow fell upon the bunk. "You awake?" he demanded. When he got no answer, his hand fell on the prisoner's shoulder and shook him. "Come on, you! I never hit you that hard. Don't try to possum me!"

Jim Branch groaned as he gave limply to the shaking. He let his eyes open and grimaced as though with pain. Teal grunted in satisfaction. "That's more like it!" There was a whisper of metal against leather; Branch couldn't avoid stiffening as the hard, cold muzzle of a sixgun was pressed against the side of his neck.

"You made a mistake," the man said harshly, "not using your gun when you had the draw on me. Hell, I told you I'd as soon kill you as not. Give me any excuse, and I will—and Vern Paxman can go hang. Understand?" Face pressed against the blanket and the gunmuzzle hard against his neck, Branch managed a nod. The gun was removed.

"I got orders to take you down to Tomahawk," Denver Teal said. "Don't try anything stupid while I cut you loose...." A knifeblade went to work, sawing at the ropes pinioning the prisoner's wrists and ankles to the frame of the bunk. When he was free Branch heard Teal's peremptory order: "Now, get up!"

Painfully he rolled to a sit on the edge of the bunk. The ache in his skull, the stiffness of his limbs, the throb of that wounded arm were things he didn't have to dissemble; still, he deliberately gave the impression of being in worse shape than he actually was. He swayed a little, head hanging. He put up a hand and touched his hurt arm, let it fall again.

His hat and coat were tossed onto the bed beside him. Denver Teal's hand struck his shoulder roughly. "Put those on. Damn it, I think you heard me!" With a curse the other man clamped down on Jim Branch's shoulder and hauled him to his feet. He came up staggering loosely; he grabbed for the frame of the upper bunk, deliberately missed and reeled against the other man. Teal cursed and stepped away.

Jim Branch's right fist, carrying all the strength he'd been able to hoard in thse moments since waking, arced around and took the man on the side of the face.

The blow had little enough steam in it, but it caught Teal by surprise. A startled sound broke from him as the blow splatted home. Branch followed through with two long steps, cocking that fist again and unleashing a second blow that struck solidly. Teal's head snapped back; his mouth fell open under the sandy moustache and he toppled and went down in a heap. Branch, with only one arm that wasn't too stiff and sore to use, could not have broken his fall if he wanted to.

He grabbed briefly at the frame of the bunk to steady himself. After that he was catching up his coat and shrugging into it, teeth gritted against the pain of that hurt arm, and pulling on his hat. He saw his Colt lying on the table and, palming it, crossed quickly to the door. He stepped out, pulling the panel shut behind him to close away the lamplight.

A wind that smelled of rain blew against him, and there was a fretful flickering of lightning. The horse Crane had ridden up from Tomahawk headquarters stood before the door, and yonder at the corral the puncher had another one saddled and was working at the third. He didn't glance around and Branch didn't bother him. Instead he took the reins of the waiting horse and led it quietly around the corner of the shack, out of sight of the corral. There, having holstered his gun, he mounted, favoring that bullet-scored shoulder that was growing painfully stiff. Still keeping the shack between him and the corral, he started to ride away at a walk, pointing toward the nearest black band of timber.

He had gone no more than a few yards when the door he had closed suddenly burst open; an angry yell split the stillness.

Branch looked back, saw Denver Teal come staggering out into the square of lampglow thrown from the open door—apparently he hadn't hit the man as hard as he thought. On the instant he gave the horse a kick, lifted it into a lope. The quick break of hoofsound brought another yell, and now a gun opened up behind him.

Not answering the fire, Jim Branch put all his attention instead on urging his borrowed mount toward those trees that were still some twenty yards ahead, etched blackly by the lightning flashes. Behind him Denver Teal was working his sixgun and shouting his rage, and in another moment Crane would undoubtedly be joining him.

Suddenly the horse broke stride, staggered and then went on. It might have stumbled over something but Branch didn't think so. He was sure the animal had been hit.

A grassed-over creekbed opened in front of him, without warning. The horse plunged over the edge of the bank and Branch felt it lose its footing; he leaped clear as they both went spilling down the shallow drop. At the bottom he landed full on the hurt arm and felt agony shoot all through him, but at least he had avoided being brained by one of those frantically struggling hooves. He lay still for a moment, before gathering his strength and climbing to his feet.

The horse had scrambled up but was standing hipshot, head hanging, favoring its off hind leg; Branch saw a black, glistening wetness and, touching the animal's rump, he felt the warm blood. It was only a shallow and glancing bullet-gouge; still, this horse could not be ridden far in such shape. Even as he stood debating, he heard a pound of hooves nearing. His head jerked up; he was feeling to see if his gun was still in the holster as he stepped clear of the injured animal.

Only one rider was coming, all out, in a reckless dash to overtake him. His guess was that it would be Denver Teal, grabbing the horse Crane had already succeeded in saddling. Branch waited, but it was only for a moment; then abruptly the horse loomed above him, a gigantic shape on the edge of the gully. On its back, bareheaded, the shape of Denver Teal showed in the constant shuttering of lightning. Teal had managed to pull up in time to keep from spilling down the bank. Now he saw Branch; his mount reared under a sudden startled jerk of his hand on the rein. Gunmetal glinted.

Once before, facing this man who'd stopped

Nick Roddy from murdering him, Jim Branch had held his fire and lived to regret it; now he thought any debt he had owed was canceled. This time he shot, and he shot to kill. Teal's gunmuzzle smeared with flame but it was a wasted bullet, which streaked off somewhere into the windy darkness. Teal was smashed from the saddle, hit the edge of the gully and slid down the drop like a half-stuffed rag doll. Jim Branch didn't have to look at him to know he was dead. He holstered the Colt.

Teal's horse started to curvet and turn away from the edge of the gully. Quicker than he had moved in a long time, Branch scrambled up the bank and with a lucky grab caught the flying reins and held it back. He threw a look over toward the line shack. Crane would be there still, with a horse probably saddled by this time. He should be coming at any minute.

Jim Branch could only hope that when he saw what had happened to Denver Teal, he'd be discouraged from trying to push this any further, alone. For his own part, he wanted no more of it. His head throbbed; his arm was hurting badly and one killing was enough. He found the stirrup, pulled himself with real effort into the saddle of the captured horse. He eased him down over the drop and then, without another look at Denver Teal, followed the gully at a walk until it carried him into the trees. There, grimly, he set to work to lose himself as the wind brought him the first cold streaks of knifing rain.

VII

THE THUNDERSTORM that had blown in to soak this upland region played itself out before morning, but Jim Branch stayed where he was—in a shallow overhang, which served as a kind of shelter except when the constant churning of the wind blew the rain directly in at him. He had had a good soaking, and his arm ached and so did his skull; he was thoroughly lost in unfamiliar territory, where he would only flounder helplessly if he tried to travel. Fortunately there was a yellow slicker lashed down behind the saddle of the borrowed horse. He made himself as comfortable in this as he could, and waited out the wet and interminable night.

He slept fitfully, waking at last in a chill dawn. At least the rain seemed over, and the cloud cover that hid the sky was beginning to break. Jim Branch climbed stiffly again into the saddle of the horse he had taken from the dead Denver Teal—it was a sorrel, wearing Vern Paxman's Tomahawk brand. He debated his next move.

Likely enough he could find again the place where he had seen those Caufield steers being driven, yesterday, but too much time had been lost and there was the storm since then, which would have washed out all sign. So, reluctantly—because those stolen steers interested him very much—he gave up any thought of them for now. His best move was to find his way down from these hills and, if possible, have something done about that arm. He started out, riding blind but feeling that if he bore east he should eventually find a way into Holster Basin.

Presently he struck a game trail; following it, he found the hills breaking and by midmorning came out upon a point that gave him, dramatically, his first sight of the Basin itself. It lay green and dun before him, spreading out toward more hills on the east—good rangeland, he noted with a stab of something very like envy; fresh now from the rain, and dotted with broken cloud shadow.

He studied it for a time, while his horse had a breather, trying to spot the features of the crude map that Wes Caufield had rough-sketched for him, and that he'd been careful to commit to memory. When he thought he had the general shape of things worked out, he rode on again, trusting the trail he followed to bring him to lower country.

Sometime before noon he rode the sorrel along the bank of a creek, through a belt of timber that thinned and showed him a ranch layout directly before him. A nice-looking spread, he noticed with approval as he approached—good, tight buildings,

THE PAXMAN FEUD

adequate corrals and work area, the whole appearing kept up and in good shape.

He didn't miss the Seven Cross brand, burnt into a slab of varnished pine wood that swung from the high gate.

Jim Branch rode in under the gate, holding the sorrel to a walk. He saw a pencil line of smoke rising from the chimney of the main house, which was a neat-looking structure of log and fieldstone with a bed of flowers, carefully tended, at the foot of the veranda that stretched across the front of it. A couple of horses, unsaddled in one of the pens, were, for the moment, the only signs of life.

Then, to his right, a voice spoke sharply: "Stop right there, fella. And don't do nothing sudden. I got a rifle pointed at your ear!"

Branch drew the sorrel to a stand and lifted both hands away from his body, the right one holding the reins. Looking straight ahead, he asked calmly, "Does that suit you?"

The voice snarled at him. "Nothing will suit me, but to see every damn one of you Tomahawk killers cleaned out of the basin. I wouldn't mind a hell of a lot starting now—with you!"

Branch turned his head, then, and found the man who stood at a corner of the corral, rifle at shoulder. He looked like a veteran cowhand, with skin burnt to bootleather by a lifetime of hard suns, and only a straggling remnant of time-whitened hair lying across his scalp. It was the apron tucked about his waist that identified him: the ranch cook.

Branch said, "I'd like to see the Caufields."

"I don't think so," the old man retorted. "That

don't seem to me noways necessary."

A bad night, a hurt arm and tender skull combined to shorten Branch's patience. "Now, look!" he said. "You're jumping to conclusions. You don't know me; you don't know that I'm a Tomahawk man."

"I got eyes, ain't I? I can see the brand on your horse! Suppose you just turn him around, and ride him back the way you—"

"It's all right, Fargo," Margie Caufield said.

She came from out a side door of the house, letting the screen swing shut behind her. She was frowning in the strong sunlight; her frown, and her voice, held uncertainty. "At least, I guess it's all right. I met this man in Latigo. So far as I know, he's not working for Tomahawk."

Fargo protested: "But, the bronc!"

"We'll give him a chance to explain that."

Her words told Branch a couple of things. For one, it looked as though his identity and his mission here in Holster Basin were being kept a secret, for now at any rate, even from the Seven Cross crew. That was all to the good. But, her own personal doubts and distrust of him still appeared as strong as when she walked out of that hotel room.

This had to be put straight, somehow; but just now he felt a trifle light-headed and in no shape to argue effectively from a saddle. He said gruffly, "Ma'am, can I get down from here?"

Fargo protested: "Don't let him, Margie! I don't care where you met him. There's no reason to trust him! And the two of us are alone here. . . ." The rifle was still leveled in the old puncher's hands, and one of them was clamped around the trigger guard. But the girl hesitated; and now, as Jim Branch turned to her, something in the way he moved and the stiffness of his handling that left arm appeared to strike home. Her eyes widening, she came a step closer.

"Are you hurt?"

"Nothing fatal. Just a sore arm—a bullet burn."

That decided her. "You had better come inside, Mister Branch," she told him, "and let me have a look. Fargo will take your horse."

"Thanks," he said, and swung stiffly down.

The old cook didn't like this arrangement at all and would have argued, but he seemed to know it would gain nothing once Margie Caufield had made up her mind. He slung his rifle across the crook of an elbow and stepped forward to take the reins, snatching them away from Branch with a look that held a potent warning. After that he stood watching as the stranger followed Margie up the path, neatly outlined with whitewashed stones, and into the house.

It was a rambling house, all on one level, that had thrown out wings as extra rooms were needed; Branch liked the pleasantly improvised air of the place. Margie Caufield led him to the kitchen, a low-ceilinged room dominated by the big, iron range that looked as though someone had only just finished working it over with blacking and polishing rag. A clock ticked somewhere; the whole peaceful quiet of the place seemed to settle about them in this room, which was the heart of any ranchhouse.

Branch said, as he hung his hat on the back of a chair, "Your brother's out with his crew?"

"What crew there is left," she told him briefly. "After Vern Paxman had his way with scaring them off." She motioned him to the table in the center of the room. "Take off your coat and let's see how that arm looks."

She had to rip away the blood-dried shirtsleeve. Her manner was coolly efficient but he could sense, from the puckering of her brows and the faint tightening of her cheeks, that she was not really calloused to the sight of a bullet wound. He apologized: "I don't like to trouble you with this, but it's a little hard to work on by myself."

The girl accepted the apology without comment; she said, after a moment, "You're lucky. That could have been a bad one. As it is you're only going to have a stiff arm for awhile."

"I've already got that," Branch said wryly, trying to make a joke of it; but she did not seem amused as she set to work, using a basin and hot water from the tea kettle on the stove, antiseptic and clean cloths to replace the crude binding job he had done. Her movements were sure and gentle, and Jim Branch submitted willingly enough, watching her with admiration as she worked. Today she was wearing a simple yellow cotton house dress, and her taffy-colored hair was pulled back and clubbed behind her neck with a bit of ribbon. She was as attractive a girl as he had ever seen.

She was naturally curious, and he couldn't refuse to enlighten her when she asked bluntly, "Who did this to you?"

"A Paxman rider. Man named Teal?"

"And—what happened to *him?*" When he hesitated she shot him a single probing look and read the answer in his face. "You killed him?"

"It was him or me."

"That's what these shootouts usually come down to, isn't it?"

If his mouth tightened then, it was not from the smart of the antiseptic she was using. "It wasn't the kind of thing you seem to think," he told her when he could trust his voice. He added, "I came here this morning because I thought your brother and I had better fill each other in on what's been happening since I last saw you. Since Wes isn't around, maybe you'd better hear my story."

"I'm afraid I'd rather not."

"I'm afraid you may have to," he said bluntly, "for there are things I've seen and heard that have a bearing on your troubles here in the Basin." She made no more objection, then, and he proceeded to relate the things that had happened to him since his departure from Latigo on Hamp Billis' freight wagon. He told her, in particular, of the Seven Cross cattle he'd seen being driven through the hills by Paxman riders. And, factually and without understatement or embellishment, he told of his capture and escape, and the killing of Denver Teal. Before he was done she had completed her work of binding the hurt arm, and she seated herself across the table to hear him out—her arms on the table, her palms folded tightly, her eyes averted. He had no way at all to judge her reaction.

There was a long stillness between them when he had finished; the busy ticking of the clock filled it. Getting no answer from the girl, Jim Branch drew a breath and said roughly, "Anyway, that should tell you a little more of the kind of men you're up against. Though I imagine it comes as no surprise."

She raised her head, at last, to look at him directly. "What will you do now?"

"Well, I have a job with Floyd Paxman, keeping an eye on his investments in the town up here. It seems a logical place to begin while I'm getting my bearings. And, it gives me an excuse for being in the Basin without giving away the fact that I'm working for Seven Cross. I'm not ready for anyone to know that yet."

"And when Tomahawk sees you there," she demanded quickly. "After what happened yesterday? How long do you think you'll last?"

He answered simply, "I hope Tomahawk has learned by now I'm not too easy disposed of. I'll watch my step and I imagine they will, too—while they try to figure me out. Meanwhile, I want to thank you for this." He indicated the expert job she had done of bandaging his hurt. "Feels like it shouldn't give me too much trouble. I'll be getting along."

He started to his feet; she rose quickly, saying, "There's nothing left of that shirt. But I think one of Wes' should just about fit you; I'll fetch it. And you look as though you could use some breakfast. When did you eat last?"

"Not lately," he admitted, and put up a hand to feel the scrape of beard stubble. "I could use a razor, if you could find me one."

"Of course. And while you're doing that I'll put together some breakfast."

"You're very kind."

She looked at him oddly. She said only, "Why, you're working for us, aren't you? It's no more

THE PAXMAN FEUD

than I should do...."

The food was good to a hungry man; but the way she watched him as he ate it was disconcerting. She seemed to be studying him as she might some kind of alien creature, and finally Branch had had enough of this. He put down his fork, and said bluntly, "Am I really poison to you? You have a way of looking at me as if I was."

Her face turned crimson, her eyes widening and her mouth falling open as she tried to stammer something. Instantly he was sorry for what he had said, but there was nothing to do but pursue it. But he softened his tone as he went on: "Wes told me something about you, Miss Caufield. About what happened to your father."

For a moment he didn't think she was going to answer, but then she found her voice. It sounded thin and strained with remembered emotion. "I was only a little girl, Mister Branch. I worshiped my father. He was the kindest and gentlest man who ever lived—a farmer who looked after his own affairs and left other men alone. But there was some trouble, something that didn't concern our family in any way. A gunman was hired and brought in to do a killing. My father was pointed out to him, by accident...."

"And the man killed him, right in front of you," Jim Branch finished. "Wes didn't tell me the rest of the story. What happened to you after that? How did you come to Holster Basin?"

"There was a cattleman," she told him, "a widower named Tom Decker. A wonderful man. He heard about us two orphans, and took us under his wing; he brought us to the Basin, to Seven

Cross. We grew up here. And when he died, a half dozen years ago, he made us his legal heirs."

"And all your life you've feared and hated anyone who reminded you of your father's killer. Anyone like me...."

Margie Caufield drew a long breath. "Mister Branch, I don't want to be unfair. Wes tells me you're no ordinary gunman, and I'm willing to take his word. But—can't you see that what I'm afraid of is the influence you may have on him? He has a reckless streak, and it wouldn't be hard to get him to take chances that would get him killed. For instance, if he knew about those steers you saw Paxman's riders driving off, yesterday, he might easily take it in his head to lead his crew over there for a showdown. And he hasn't your training, or your talent for self-preservation...."

At that moment, their talk was interrupted by sound of a horseman arriving in the yard outside. Margie said quickly, "That could be Wes," and hurried out to see.

Jim Branch deliberately finished off the last of his coffee before he followed her through the house and outside, where he found the Caufields, brother and sister, standing by the horse from which Wes had just dismounted. The young fellow turned to Branch. "What's this Margie tells me? You been taken prisoner by that Tomahawk crowd? And shot it out with one of them?"

Branch dropped down the veranda steps. "Just a little run-in," he explained briefly. "A man named Teal . . ." He went on to relate as much as he thought Wes Caufield needed to know, and was forced to answer again some of the same questions the girl had put to him.

Wes seemed alarmed by what he heard, and even more so when Jim Branch told of his arrangement with Floyd Paxman. "If you stay here with us, we can stand together. But in that town, you'll be on your own if Nick Roddy decides to bring the Tomahawk crew to finish you off. Floyd Paxman will be no help if gunplay starts."

But Jim Branch was determined. "I can do you no good here. As long as they don't know there is a connection, there's always the chance someone will tip his hand and give us what we need to work on. No, I think I'll be heading for this Sharp's Creek place, and play it from there."

Caufield shook his head, but he said, "I'll have Fargo bring up your horse."

As he walked away to see to this, Margie looked at Branch with an odd expression. "You didn't say anything to him about that stolen beef. . . ."

"You asked me not to," he pointed out. "And besides, I think you may be right: It's not the time for him to be told something that might make him lose his head."

Her eyes studied his face; then, for the first time since he had met her, a smile touched the girl's lips, and the effect was worth waiting for. It warmed her eyes and removed, briefly, the trouble that shadowed them. It showed that this girl had a face that was meant for smiling.

"Then you *do* understand," she said quietly. "Thank you, Jim."

He wanted to answer, but now the cook, Fargo, came leading the sorrel with the Tomahawk brand. So Branch satisfied himself with a nod and a look, and turned to take the reins from the old man who looked as surly and suspicious as ever. He mounted, favoring the hurt arm. "Thanks again for this," he told Margie, indicating the bandage. "And for the breakfast. Maybe we'll meet again."

And with that, he reined away and touched a spur to the sorrel. When he looked back he could still see the bright yellow of her skirt as she stood watching him ride away.

VIII

It was when he had his first look at the town of Sharp's Creek, itself, that Branch began to appreciate the investment Floyd Paxman had here. The town itself was modest enough, a couple dozen houses and business buildings, about half of logs and the other half frame, that stretched along a single wide street near the shallow mountain stream that must give the place its name. Riding in across the wagon bridge, he studied the buildings on either side of him; but as he passed along the twisted street, which was still dotted with an occasional pine tree stump where timber had been cleared for building material, he quickly saw that whatever there was to the town, it was mostly Floyd Paxman's.

The name appeared with monotonous regularity on the signs identifying the various enterprises. The grocery was his, and the grain and the feed store. So was the long, narrow building that seemed to be a bar, with rooms for rent in the back—it probably served Sharp's Creek, for the present at least, as its hotel. And finally there was an imposing new structure, roofed with shingles so new they dazzled, identified by its big lettered sign as PAXMAN'S EMPORIUM, which would appear to comprise anything else that was lacking, including the local post office and stage station.

Branch dismounted here, thinking it the likeliest place to find Paxman if he was here and not still down in Latigo. Tying the Tomahawk sorrel to one of the roof uprights, he mounted the steps to the wide double door. But with a hand on the knob, he became aware of voices somewhere around length of the porch and dropped to the ground. Beyond the store-building, he saw now, was a layout of corrals and a goodsized barn. There were mules in one of the corrals, a wagon parked nearby; apparently this was Paxman's local branch of his freight business.

The voices he'd heard belonged to a pair of men who had just emerged out of the barn. One was Floyd Paxman; the other was the muleskinner, Hamp Billis.

Seeing Billis, Branch's face took on a bleak hardness and he started toward them at an unhurried and deliberate stride. The pair had halted in the sunshine before the barn doorway—Paxman talking now, the smaller man bobbing his narrow head as he listened. Neither seemed aware of Jim Branch until the latter was a matter of a few yards distant. When finally Billis happened to look in his direction, it was possible to see the sudden change in the man's face—the eye-popping, almost frightened stare of surprise and consternation.

If he had ever had any questions about that business yesterday, when Vern Paxman's riders jumped the wagon during its stopover at the spring, they were settled by that look.

Floyd Paxman turned, then, and the astonishment that came into his bony face was clearly genuine. "Branch!" he cried. "What are you doing here?"

"I'm walking around and breathing," Jim Branch said dryly, as he came to a halt. "Which is something of a surprise, at that. I take it Billis has told you what happened to me on the way up here?"

"He's just been filling me in," Paxman said, nodding. "I got in from Latigo, myself, less than an hour ago."

The muleskinner put in—a shade too quickly, "I told him about them gunslingers of Vern's jumping us, and taking us both off guard. Mister, it was plain hell to pull out like that, and leave you there in their hands! If there'd been maybe just one fewer of the bastards . . ."

"Well," Branch said, "there is now."

"You killed one?" Paxman exclaimed.

He nodded. "Fellow they called Denver Teal. They had me tied up in a line cabin of some sort, with him guarding me. But he got a little careless."

"And you're not hurt, after all!"

"Hardly any to mention," Branch corrected him, and flexed his arm, wincing a little. "Certainly I came off better than I had any right to expect."

"Thank God for that!" the freighter exclaimed hoarsely. "I'd never have forgiven myself. The last thing I ever intended was to let you ride, without warning, into a hailstorm like that! At least, now, it's finished and done with."

Jim Branch said quietly, "Maybe not quite finished." He looked at Hamp Billis. "Could be this fellow forgot to tell you the whole story."

"What do you mean?"

The tall man's eyes were completely cold, and there were the first signs of apprehension in the muleskinner's returning stare.

"How about it? You want to tell him the rest, Billis? Or shall I?"

The man's jaw sagged; his face had lost color. His eyes shuttled back and forth between Branch and Paxman. "Afraid I dunno what you're getting at."

"You don't!" Branch turned to the freighter. "It was a setup, Paxman. They knew perfectly well I'd be riding that wagon. When they were late arriving to pick me up, he tried every way he could to stall and hold me there for them."

Hamp Billis turned livid. "A lie!" he shouted—and got the flat of Branch's palm across his jaw, so hard that his head wrenched about on his neck and his hat went tumbling. He might have been knocked off his feet if Branch hadn't caught him by a shoulder, and swung him around to face Paxman.

"Look at your boss when you say that. See if you can convince him!"

Billis was stammering wildly. "You don't believe this, do you? You wouldn't take his word, against somebody that's worked for you as long as me?"

The look in Paxman's eyes silenced him. The protests of innocence died in stammerings; his jaw

THE PAXMAN FEUD

clamped hard, until the muscles stood out in lumps beneath the lean and gray-stubbled jowls. And Floyd Paxman said coldly, "I've known, for some time, my brother had a spy planted with me; I never quite knew who it was! I guess now I do!

"Get your things together, and drift. I hate to lose a good mulehandler; but, by God, a traitor I don't need! I'll give you five minutes to get out of my town."

"*Your* town!" Hamp Billis' eyes glittered and his whole face had turned strangely mottled. He was sneering, suddenly, taking refuge in bluster. "You really think you're the big man in Holster Basin, don't you? You just wait a while. You just see what happens when—"

"That's enough!" snapped Paxman. His mouth was a stern trap as he dug a roll of bills from his pocket, peeled off a couple and flung them into the dirt in front of the man's scuffled boots. "There's your pay. Don't ever let me see your face again!" And, turning sharply on his heel, he strode away in the direction of the store building.

Hamp Billis was shaking with fury and humiliation. He looked at the money as though he could not bring himself to lean and pick it up, but, then, with a muttered obscenity, he went down and grabbed them out of the dirt, and also got the hat that had fallen from his head. As he straightened, his eye met Jim Branch's; for a long moment he held the latter with a look of pure hatred. Then his narrow chest swelled with a drawn breath and he said between his teeth, "It's fun pushing people around, ain't it? Well—enjoy it while you can!"

Branch didn't bother to answer. He stood and

watched Hamp Billis' gangling figure move away, around the corner of the store and so going from sight in the direction of the street. He turned, then, as Paxman called from the store building's rear door. Branch walked over, and followed him inside.

He found himself in a cubbyhole of a room that had been partitioned off at the rear of the building, and which appeared to serve Paxman as his local office. It had no proper furnishings, merely a kitchen table and a few straight chairs, and filing cabinets fashioned from empty crates and crammed with a jumble of papers, account books, bills of lading.

Paxman saw the other man's critical appraisal of the room and took pains to explain: "This is only temporary, you understand. I've already made my plans for putting up a business block, across the way—solid brick construction. Perhaps next year, I'll manage to get at that."

Branch, accepting the chair his employer had indicated, took out his cigar case, selected one and got it lighted. Through the smoke, he said, "No fooling. You've got ambitious ideas for this town."

"It will support them," Paxman said brusquely. "There's a fine potential in Holster Basin—if it's only allowed to develop." He began pacing the narrow confines of the room, apparently too worked up to sit; he was still fuming over the unmasking of Hamp Billis.

"This explains so much!" he burst out after a moment. "Vern seemed to know every move I made, almost as soon as I made it. I'm convinced he learned somehow that I offered to help young

Caufield with a loan. I think that has to be the reason Nick Roddy was sent to kill him at the depot, two days ago—they were afraid Caufield might be planning to accept my offer, and then it would be too late." He flung out a hand in agitation. "Branch, you've no idea what it means to a man when he knows the evil he fights is his own brother!"

Branch could think of no answer for that, and he sat and puffed on his cigar; and after a moment Paxman himself changed the subject. "Anyway, I'm glad that no worse came of your adventure on the way up from Latigo; at least I see, now, just what lengths they'll go to. I could hardly blame you if you'd taken the month's pay I gave you, and simply ridden out of this proposition!"

Jim Branch lifted a shoulder. "I'm still here."

"And you'll be wanting a place to stay," the other man said, nodding. "One of the things we need is an adequate hotel. I've had plans drawn for one; but at present the only rooms to be had are in the rear of the saloon. They're not much, I'm afraid. Tell Durkin I said to give you your pick."

"All right." Branch eased to his feet. "I had my warbag in your wagon, when we were jumped yesterday. Do you have any idea what might have become of it?"

"It's in the barn. I never touched it; though I can't guarantee what Hamp Billis might have done." He added, "Get your room; get the feel of the town. I'll be talking to you later." His shrewd glance had noticed the bandage bulking under the sleeve of the other's jacket. "We have no doctor here, as yet; but if that arm needs looking at, Ed

Troy at the livery is a good hand with bullet wounds."

"It feels fine," Branch assured him, and went out to hunt for his belongings.

Everything seemed intact. Though it was almost certain Hamp Billis would have seized the chance to plow through the carpetbag, Branch had left nothing in it to tell Vern Paxman of his connection with the Caufields; and none of his possessions were missing. He carried the carpetbag around front to where the sorrel was tied, got the latter and led it down the street to the livery stable. He left the animal in care of Ed Troy, a balding, stoop-shouldered man who operated one of the few independent businesses in Floyd Paxman's town, and who looked askance at the Tomahawk brand on the stranger's horse but asked no questions. Afterward Jim Branch turned across the dusty street to the saloon to find himself a room.

There was no trace of Hamp Billis. He could only suppose that Vern Paxman's spy, having been exposed, was already on his way to report at Tomahawk....

The man behind the bar—Durkin—had a head like a cannonball, close-cropped red hair, and a paunchy middle and two ham-like forearms, one with an anchor tattooed on its hairy back. He heard the message from Floyd Paxman and told Branch to take his pick of the rooms, all of which happened to be empty. Jim Branch chose the one at the very end of the long and narrow building.

He could stand in the center of the room and narrowly miss touching all four walls. There was a wooden bunk, a single straight chair, a rickety table with a lamp on it, and a mirror with a crack across the middle. A row of hooks on the unpapered wall served as the closet. The window, propped open by a stick, looked out on weeds and trash that stretched clear to the line of willows and alder along the creek. The door had no latch.

Jim Branch had seen better-looking cribs in the redlight districts of Kansas cowtowns.

He was in no position to be choosy, however; and just now, standing alone in the quiet of the little cubicle, it occurred to him that he was dog-tired. He had had no real rest in the misery camp he had made in the rain last night, and the hurt arm and loss of blood had drained him. He dropped his carpetbag, hung up his hat and coat, put his gun and belt on the chair beside the bunk and pulled off his boots. Trying not to think about the possibility of wild life in the musty-smelling bedding, he stretched out and almost immediately was asleep.

A rumble of voices and tramp of boots roused him. Lying there, not yet fully awake, he puzzled it out and realized that the sounds he heard were in the barroom, at the far front end of the long building; but they were funneled right back through the thin walls and the floorboards that ran lengthwise to act as a perfect sounding board. Leather bootheels boomed hollowly, and voices came as an indistinct rumble.

It must be dandy trying to sleep in here on a Saturday night, when Durkin had a drinking crowd on his hands. Just now, he judged it was the early part of the afternoon—he could only have slept an hour or so—there were perhaps a half dozen men up front in the bar. The voices sounded to him like angry ones. Something about them moved him to lever into a sitting position, reaching for his boots. He drew them on and stood, buckling his gunbelt into place. After that he was at the door, listening, and then slipped through into the dark hallway that stretched the length of the building.

Here the voices fairly boomed down the hall at him, mingling and distorted; he recognized Floyd Paxman's, and thought he heard the rumbling tones of Nick Roddy. Hand on gun he started forward, moving quickly and stealthily toward the door at the front end of the hallway.

He had almost reached it when he heard his own name, rising above the ruck of garbled speech; and then the bartender, Durkin, said clearly in a voice that shook with fear: "Take that damn gun out of my middle, Roddy! I ain't hiding him. He's in the room at the far end. Go look for yourselves...."

Quickly drawing his gun, Branch slipped through the door to one of the empty cubicles, which stood ajar at his elbow. Pressing against the wall, he waited, and, an instant later, boots were tramping past his hiding place. He had a glimpse through the crack of Nick Roddy and the puncher named Crane, both carrying guns. The boots came to a halt; a door slammed open with a force that shook the whole flimsy length of the wall where Jim Branch rested his shoulder.

A moment's silence, and after that the tramp of boots was rolling forward again. "Ain't there," Nick Roddy announced. "There's some stuff that could be his, but not him."

Durkin cried out quickly: "He must have used the back door, then—I never saw him come through this way. That's the truth!"

His protest must have carried conviction. Branch heard Vern Paxman say, "I guess we have to scout the town and dig him out."

"Hell!" Nick Roddy grunted. "Easier to burn him out."

"*Burn—?*" That was Floyd's cry—a strangled outburst of horror. "You don't mean it! You wouldn't dare!"

Jim Branch had moved stealthily back out into the hall. Through the opening at the forward end he could look directly into the bar, and now he saw Floyd Paxman and his bartender, Durkin, confronted by the three from Tomahawk.

It was the first time he had observed the Paxman brothers together. The contrast with the rancher's solid frame made Floyd seem gaunter, more hollow-chested than ever; yet the family resemblance was clearly there. Just now, Floyd's face looked drained of color as Nick Roddy told him, on a note of heavy mockery, "You know, you was warned what could happen if you kept getting in the way. Ain't that so, Chief?"

Vern nodded his massive head, the inevitable cigar making a cloud of blue smoke about his jaws. "Yes, dear brother. You most certainly were. I've been patient; but now that you bring in a hired tough, and set him to killing off my men—"

"I never hired him to do killing," Floyd Paxman protested.

"All the same, Red Shober and Denver Teal are both dead!"

Roddy couldn't keep silent for long. The muzzle of the gun in his hand wheeled dangerously as he muttered, "This fellow needs a lesson, Chief! That brand-new store building, now—it ought to burn real good, for a start."

"Maybe, Vern Paxman was not to be hurried; his nod was thoughtful, speculative, abstracted. "Maybe..."

"No!" Floyd cried hoarsely. "*No!*" He even started toward his brother. At once, Crane stepped in and his shoulder struck the freighter, flung him back. A heavy table scraped floorboards as he half fell against it.

Vern hadn't moved. He was looking at Floyd with a thoughtful expression on his craggy face. Now he spoke to his men: "The pair of you—get out. We want to talk...."

Branch thought Nick Roddy was going to protest; he saw the thick chest swell, but, with the next breath, Roddy's ugly face changed expression in a way that was most odd. The upper lip pulled back, showing his teeth in what was plainly a grin; the eyes narrowed to cunning slits. He nodded. "Sure. I get you!" And swung away toward the street door, with a jerk of his head at the puzzled Crane.

Then Vern took of his hat and dropped it on the table beside him. To the bartender, he said gruffly, "Give us a bottle and a couple of glasses here—and then, go lose yourself."

These items were standing on the bar in easy reach. Quickly, Durkin grabbed them up and brought them over; under Vern's muddy stare he placed the liquor and glasses on the table and, then, whipping off his apron, threw it on the bar where it hit and slid to the floor. Letting it lie, Durkin hurried out through the swinging doors.

The barroom was left to the Paxman brothers, and to the one who hovered unseen in the dark hallway.

IX

IT COULD BE a very interesting family scene that was about to take place, and Jim Branch wished he could stay for it. But he had a strong hunch he was needed elsewhere, just then, and with regret he turned away. Chairs were being pulled out from the table and boots scraped floorboards as the brothers seated themselves; glass clinked on glass. These small sounds helped cover the noise he wasn't entirely able to keep from making as he retreated down the hallway. He gained the door at its far end, seemingly undetected, and let himself through.

A drowsy afternoon lay upon the town, seeming to hush the murmur of the creek that ran behind the buildings, even stilling the whisper of wind in pineheads and twinkling cottonwoods. At a rear corner of the saloon, Branch peered forward and saw the ring of horses tied to a big pine near the street. He counted six, which gave him an idea of the odds; but at the moment there were no Tomahawk men in sight. Jim Branch left his place and went at a sprint across the open toward the rear of the next building.

He reached it without hearing anything to indicate he'd been seen; he could breathe easier now as he moved on to approach the peak-roofed livery stable, which stood just beyond.

Ed Troy was cleaning out his stalls; he came from a side doorway, tooling a wheelbarrow with a pitchfork standing thrust upright into its steaming load. He lowered the wheelbarrow and straightened his stooped, narrow shape. Branch veered toward him.

"What's going on?" he demanded with a scowl. "I seen that Tomahawk crowd. Is anything afoot?"

"You might say so," Branch agreed, nodding briefly. "I got an idea Vern Paxman's crew is about to put your town to the torch."

The pale eyes widened. "That's a poor joke!"

"You don't see me laughing."

At that Troy stiffened, straightening his stoop-shouldered frame; his lantern jaw settled. "By God, there are some in this town that resent being used for the ambitions of them Paxman brothers—either of them! This was our town and our home, before they laid greedy hands on Holster Basin!"

This was interesting. Branch caught him up on it. "You talk as if you think Floyd Paxman has things at heart other than the good of the Basin."

"Hell!" The gaunt shoulders lifted in a shrug. Troy said, "He talks good—but he's a Paxman, ain't he? Where that pair's concerned I figure it's six of one, half dozen of the other."

"Well, I suggest you keep your eyes open—because you're apt to see some sparks flying in about a minute!" Branch ducked inside the barn, moved quickly toward the wide street door, where he paused, just inside, to cast an appraising look over the town. Everything was quiet for the moment, almost no life showing except for the horses tethered outside the bar. Then, in front of the raised stoop of Floyd Paxman's big store building he saw two more that stood on trailing reins. One of them resembled the bay Nick Roddy had ridden yesterday up in the hills. . . .

Immediately Branch walked out of the livery into the smash of the sun. There were some twenty yards to cover, at an angle across the full width of the street, to where new roof shingles atop Floyd Paxman's store made a brilliant dazzle. Hand on holstered gun, he expected any moment to hear a shout as a Tomahawk man saw him out there, but the seconds passed and nothing happened.

Now he was near enough that he could hear activity inside the store building—the sound of men tromping about, laughing and talking, and once, a crash, as though something heavy had been overturned. Branch swung wide around the two saddle horses, drawing his gun, and moved directly up the plank steps to the porch.

There was a gurgling sound of liquid being poured freely from a container, and through the screen door a sudden, penetrating odor of kerosene hit him in the face. He found the handle of the door and as he pulled it wide, it squealed on its stiff new spring. Hoping that the swift transition from brilliant daylight to interior gloom would not spell a disadvantage, he slipped in.

It was darker in there, all right, but he blinked rapidly to help his eyes adjust. The place was being turned into a wreck as fast as Crane and Roddy could manage it. A display of hardware had been kicked over and merchandise was scattered over the floor; one counter was tilted against the shelves behind it. And yonder, Nick Roddy, with his back to the door, was reaching up to sweep another shelf clean.

Here too was Crane, just tossing aside the kerosene tin he'd emptied. Neither man seemed aware yet of a newcomer, they were making too much noise themselves and having too good a time. Even as Branch got his bearings, he saw the spurt of flame as Crane snapped a match to life on his thumbnail and held it poised.

At the first word from Branch the flaming match would have dropped and Floyd Paxman's store would have been a blazing furnace. He saw only one chance of preventing that, and he took it. He moved the barrel of his gun, and let the hammer fall.

The explosion of the gun smashed its concussion against the walls. As intended, his bullet struck Crane in the hip and spun him; thus, when the match flew from his fingers it landed harmlessly in the wide aisle splitting the middle of the room. Branch, walking forward into the stinging balloon of smoke from the gun's muzzle, deliberately set one boot upon the burning stick.

Crane had tumbled full-length and was twisting and moaning on the floor. A glance satisfying him that the man was not seriously hurt, Jim Branch lifted his eyes and the muzzle of his gun, then, toward Nick Roddy.

The big fellow had jerked about and was reaching for his gun. Branch fired again, in warning. That stopped the move, and he said crisply, "Leave it alone, Nick. Unfasten the belt and drop it." When Roddy made no effort to comply, anger welled inside Branch and he raised the weapon slightly. "If I have to use this gunbarrel on you once more," he said harshly, "I swear this time I'll bust your head! See if I don't!"

Angry color flooded up from Roddy's throat into his flat cheeks and even to his ears, leaving his forehead oddly pale and mottled by contrast. A single, ugly word broke past his lips. Then, with savage movements, he jerked at the leather tongue of his gunbelt, freed it from the buckle prong and flung belt and holster from him, to clatter against a stack of new tin pails and send them rolling. He faced Branch and the level gun—his shoulders rolled slightly forward, his head sunk, his furious stare waiting.

Jim Branch backed away, keeping the weapon between them. He flicked a look around at the wreckage that had been made of Floyd Paxman's place of business; he smelled the eyesmarting reek of kerosene, mingled with the powder stink, and he shook his head. "You trying to hurt Paxman? Or do you just like to destroy things? I don't think Vern gave you any orders to do this."

Roddy said roughly, "The hell with what you think! One of these times, mister—"

"Oh, shut up!"

Crane was not too badly hurt, despite the fact he

was bleeding profusely and groaning as though in mortal agony. Branch knelt and lifted the gun from his holster and flipped it away; after that he straightened and told Nick Roddy, "All right—take him out of here."

The big man hesitated, then shrugged and started forward, Branch keeping carefully out of his way. Roddy hooked a hand under Crane's armpit and lifted him to his feet, but as soon as his weight hit that hurt leg Crane collapsed with a groan. Roddy, swearing, let him go down.

Jim Branch wasn't to be put off. In the same tone he said, "You heard me. Get him out. Carry him, if you have to."

As it turned out, Nick Roddy had to. Cursing steadily, he leaned and got a fireman's hold on the wounded man and came up with him riding his broad shoulders. A stagger and shift to get his weight distributed, and the big fellow went striding out of the building, not seeming much hampered by his burden. He batted the screen door open and tramped outside, and Branch was close behind him.

Holding at the top of the steps, where he had a vantage and a better view, Branch watched as Roddy stooped and let Crane slide from his shoulders to the ground. The man groaned and cursed him and Roddy said, with little sympathy, "You ain't that hurt. Shut up!" Branch lifted his glance, then, keenly alert; for he saw what looked like the whole town beginning to converge on him, drawn by the sound of gunfire.

Yonder, the cluster of Tomahawk men outside the bar had been joined by both the Paxmans, who emerged to stand a moment staring in Branch's direction and then were starting toward him across the dusty width of the street. From other buildings other men, townspeople, were moving up—somewhat more cautiously; it was as though they all traveled the spokes of a wheel, the steps of the big store building its hub. But it was Vern Paxman's riders who presented the danger, and as he waited for them he was keenly alert, the gun levered and ready.

Floyd Paxman lifted an anxious voice, his words coming sharp and thin in the stillness: "Branch! Man, what's going on? What was the shooting?"

Jim Branch answered while letting his careful attention range over the Tomahawk men. "I think you better have a look," he said, and moved aside for him as Floyd broke forward in a trot.

The crowd had gathered by now. There were maybe a dozen townspeople, not counting the kids and dogs, and even a few women who hung in the background—looking on with scared faces, one or two with children clutching their skirts. Among the men Branch saw Ed Troy, the livery owner; Troy had picked himself up a shotgun somewhere. And there was a brawny looking man in a blacksmith's leather apron, the soot of his tempering fire still black on face and muscled arms, a big hogleg revolver tucked behind his belt. Branch thought he glimpsed another gun, as well. But for the moment all these people were holding their distance—concerned but cautious, taking no part.

Crane still lay on his back in the dirt where he'd been placed, his eyes closed and blood leaking from his wound. Nick Roddy stood over him, acid stare lifted to Branch, never wavering from the face of the man he hated. So far no one was challenging the leveled sixshooter.

The spring of the screen door squealed stiffly; on the threshold, Floyd Paxman halted as the strong odor of kerosene, and the sight of destruction within, hit him like a blow in the face. "It was Roddy and his friend," Branch explained. "They were all ready to set a match to it, when I stopped them."

Slowly, Floyd backed away, letting the screen slam shut. He turned; he looked sick with horror and anger, the sagging folds of his cadaverous cheeks trembling to the violent shaking of his head. His stare sought his brother's face. "By God!" he cried hoarsely. "Has it really come to this? Are you asking for a showdown?"

Branch, carefully watching Vern Paxman, was surprised and puzzled at the flicker of alarm he thought he saw cross the cowman's blocky features. Vern spoke a little too quickly: "Don't be a damn fool! I didn't order this. The boys got a little over-anxious."

"Not at all," Jim Branch corrected him. "They were having themselves a hell of a good time. I almost hated to break up their fun." Vern gave him a black look.

Floyd Paxman was ridden still by the outrage of what had been done to his store. "Who's going to pay for this?" he demanded. "They deliberately ruined half my stock! You want to see for yourself the mess they made?"

"No, I don't want to see it," Vern answered. He seemed to have recovered from his momentary loss of aplomb. "Figure up the damage and let me know."

"Don't worry!" Floyd snapped. "I most certainly will."

"And don't *you* worry, dear brother! When I finally decide your town is ripe for the torch—you'll know it. And it'll take more than any one man to stop me!"

Vern's cold eye settled again on Jim Branch as he said that. Branch returned the look with a shake of his head. "You know, you might be in for a surprise. There are people who call this town and this Basin their home. I think they may be getting tired of letting themselves be shoved around in a private fight between the two of you."

For the first time Vern Paxman seemed aware they had an audience. He looked around him, at the faces of the men of Sharp's Creek; he saw the bleak expressions on those faces, and the guns that a few of them were carrying. If Ed Troy and the blacksmith and the others made no menacing gesture with their weapons, neither did they break gaze. They returned the cowman's stare, unflinching, and it seemed to Jim Branch that Paxman's own look underwent a subtle change as he saw this display of determination. His expression grew a shade more thoughtful, became edged with caution.

The Tomahawk owner lifted his shoulders in a heavy shrug. "This is a lot of fuss over nothing," he said gruffly. "Nobody's burning any town. It was never anything but a kind of a joke, between my dear brother and me. Maybe just now, it did get out of hand. . . ."

"A real funny joke," Jim Branch observed dryly. "I bet you two have had lots of laughs over it!"

Suddenly Nick Roddy had had too much. Angry speech burst from him: "Hell, boss! Why do you argue with him? We come here to get this bird. Then, let's get him!"

Jim Branch simply let the sixgun barrel in his hand swing and settle on the big man. "You want to start it, friend?" he suggested.

And now, in the sudden quiet, the snick of a shotgun's twin hammers going back to full cock was startlingly loud. Ed Troy's scattergun was pointed casually at the clump of Tomahawk riders; and beside him, the big blacksmith now pulled his hogleg revolver from behind his belt. As undramatically as that—without a word spoken—these men of Sharp's Creek ranged themselves with Jim Branch; without warning, the Tomahawk crew found itself caught and immobilized by a threat of determined men and leveled guns.

Vern Paxman saw the situation, and, though his scowl was dangerous, he was wise enough to let the challenge go. He shrugged again. "We'll settle nothing this way." He singled out a couple of his riders. "You two stay with Crane. Fix him up so he can ride, and bring him in with you. The rest, get your horses."

He was already turning away, moving with a solid stride; there was certainly nothing about him to suggest he had just sustained a bad defeat. He did not even look back when Nick Roddy shouted once, and then fell silent in furious, baffled anger.

It was over as quickly as that. Tomahawk was gone, the crowd dispersed, the stillness of late summer lying once more undisturbed on this town of Sharp's Creek. Crane, groggy and groaning with the pain of his bullet-skewered leg, had been hefted onto his horse and led away, swaying groggily and clinging to the saddlehorn. Jim Branch, having watched them out of sight, turned and walked into the store.

The sight and smell of the place pulled down his mouth in a sour grimace. He rummaged around, found the two Colt revolvers that Crane and Roddy had been forced to leave behind, and carried them into the rear room; there, in the dingy surroundings of his temporary office, Floyd Paxman sat at the table with a bottle before him and a kitchen tumbler half full of whisky in his hand. He looked positively green; his clothing hung on him and the skin seemed to hang in folds upon his scrawny throat. He lifted the tumbler, tossed the whisky off and shuddered as it went down. He dropped his hand back onto the tabletop and stared straight in front of him, at nothing.

There was no hint of offering Jim Branch a drink.

Branch laid the captured guns on the table. He said, "The stink in this building is terrible. You better get the mess cleaned up and that kerosene washed out, or something could set it off even yet."

"Yes ... yes!" Paxman wagged his head, an impatient gesture. If Branch expected any thanks for what he had done this afternoon, he wasn't to get it. He stood looking down at the man for a moment, frowning with puzzled thoughts.

It was all very odd. Here was Floyd, a man he knew to be a physical coward, seeking courage from a bottle and trembling in the aftermath of that encounter. Ranged against him had been the full weight of Vern Paxman's Tomahawk and Vern Paxman's tough crew—and yet, somehow, Branch had gained a definite impression that Floyd carried the upper hand. It hadn't been solely Jim Branch's gun that made the difference, nor even the weapons of the townsmen backing him up. No; in spite of all Tomahawk's bluster, there was some power possessed by Floyd Paxman that his brother knew he had to reckon with, and which held matters at a draw. It puzzled him, and it forced him to look at this frightened man before him with considerably more respect, even if he failed to understand.

There were plainly no answers to be had from Floyd, who was helping himself now to another drink, the neck of the bottle chattering against the tumbler. Baffled, Jim Branch reached for a cigar as he pondered. He was about to strike a match when he remembered, and, turning with a shudder, walked out of that place with its reek and danger of spilled kerosene before he struck up his smoke.

Standing on the steps in front of the store he got his cigar going, drew deep of the smoke as he looked over the quiet town. The sun was dragging lower; there was the first feel of coming evening. No trace remained of the encounter that had taken place here, other than a spot of blood darkening the ground where Crane had laid wounded.

That reminded Branch of the used shells still in his gun. He took it from the leather, and proceeded to refill the chambers.

X

THAT NIGHT another storm swept the high hills. Lying in his uncomfortable bed, Jim Branch listened to the rumor of thunder rumbling away off there and was consumed by impatience and a sense of small accomplishment. Certainly, he'd been busy enough since he stepped off the train at Latigo station two days ago: two men dead, and himself deeply involved in the affairs of Holster Basin. But in his main purpose—the effort to be of use to the Caufields—he couldn't see that he was getting anywhere.

He rose in the morning with his mind made up on a course of action. The day was clear, brisk; remains of the storm hung in cloud tatters about the higher peaks, but the rest of the sky was swept clean by a wind that pummeled the cottonwoods along Sharp's Creek, bringing through the window a feel of changing seasons.

In this high country, even in the heart of summer, fall was no more than a few weeks away.

Branch found that his hurt arm was scarcely stiff at all, bothering him little as he shaved and dressed—this was a pleasant discovery, and helped ease his sour temper. He strapped on gun and belt, drew on his hat and walked out through the long tunnel of hallway and past the bar at the front, barely nodding to the greeting that Durkin, Floyd Paxman's bartender, gave him.

From Paxman himself he had had no word since that business at the store, yesterday afternoon—the way the freighter had been belting his liquor away, it seemed likely he was nursing a whale of a hangover. This encouraged Jim Branch to go about his own plans, having no other orders.

One more thing Sharp's Creek really needed was a decent place to get a meal. The eat shack here was inferior even to the one in Latigo, a hole-in-the-wall with four hard stools lining a plain plank counter, the air swimming blue with burnt grease. Branch had a breakfast of watery potatoes and half-fried ham and eggs, and coffee so thick it all but floated his spoon. Afterward he went up the street to the livery barn. On the way, he twice encountered citizens of the town who nodded and spoke to him with considerable respect. And arriving at the barn, he saw the look of sudden alarm that showed itself on Ed Troy's face.

"You ain't leaving us? You want the sorrel?"

"I got a little ride to make," Branch said. "But I'll be back. And I think I'd just as soon have another horse besides the sorrel." He felt uneasily vulnerable, forking the Tomahawk animal—it seemed an invitation for trouble, an open defiance of Vern Paxman.

Ed Troy sounded relieved to know he meant to return. "There's a nice stockinged roan out in the corral: I can let you have him reasonable if you just want him for the day. He's getting fat; he can use the exercise. A good, sound animal—good wind and bottom. Take you anywhere."

"Let's have a look at him."

The roan looked all right and they agreed to terms. The liveryman ran him out of the corral, and Branch put his gear on him. As he finished he saw that Herb Mattox, the blacksmith, had come up and was leaning against a post to watch. The big man had gone out of his way to speak to Branch the night before; now he returned the latter's greeting. "Thought for a minute you was leaving us for good," he said, echoing Ed Troy's sentiments. "But Ed, here, says you ain't. Glad to hear that. Tell you the truth, Branch, after yesterday we all feel more comfortable with you around."

Branch finished taking up the cinch, smoothed the stirrup leather as he looked closely from one man to the other. His answer was blunt. "I wouldn't know why. I'm working for Floyd Paxman—not for you."

"We're aware of that," Mattox said, wagging his massive head. "And we can't help but wish it was otherwise. Us folks here in Sharp's Creek have got no money to speak of. Otherwise, we'd be tempted to try and hire you away from Floyd, to look after the town's interests."

Irritation made him speak shortly. "Nothing I can do for you, that you can't do as well for yourselves! If you people don't like being shoved around by the Paxmans, then you've just got to start shoving back. That's what you did yesterday, and you looked pretty good doing it."

But he could tell, from their expressions, this wasn't what either man wanted to hear him say. They wanted a champion—at the very least, a leader. They were no braver nor any bigger cowards, no wiser nor more shortsighted, than the run of men anywhere; let someone else walk out in front, and if their interests were at stake they might even follow him into danger. But no one wanted to go first.

He didn't try to argue. He mounted up and reined away, leaving the pair of them to draw whatever wisdom they could from what he had told them.

Crossing the wagon bridge, he struck directly north across the Basin. It was still not very familiar ground and he rode warily, keeping off the ridges and studying every open stretch before he crossed it; he knew he would be fair game for Nick Roddy or, likely enough, for any other of the Tomahawk crowd he might happen onto. Once he sighted a pair of horsemen as they came down off a hogback and vanished into the willows along a watercourse. It was too far to see their faces or even to read the brands on their horses. He took no chances, but drew rein in a clump of scrub pine until they were clearly gone.

Traveling in this cautious way, he could only chafe at the time he was spending. But at last the ground began to lift, and as the bare rock and timber closed in he felt his tension ease somewhat. Here in the hills there was still danger, but a man had a better chance. Besides, he had ridden them enough by now—alone, and as the prisoner of Tomahawk—that he thought he had their general pattern clear. With certain high landmarks as guideposts he was sure that, by rough triangulation, he could find again the line cabin where he'd killed Denver Teal.

But he had lost enough time, and, not wanting to retrace that much ground, he took the chance of swinging north and west, trusting to memory and an outdoorsman's instincts. Sure enough, he presently found himself in country that looked familiar, and before much longer was certain he had struck the route he and his captors followed when they brought him in. Pushing on, he was shortly rewarded when he hit upon the very thing he had been looking for—that sparsely timbered draw where they had met a run of stolen Caufield cattle.

It had rained twice, since, and low-hanging cloud tatters that occasionally swallowed up the sun indicated it could happen again. But, although he had known there was a good chance all sign of the stolen beef would have been washed out, he still wanted a try at least at tracking them. In hill country, after all, the lay of the land itself limited the choice for a man driving cattle.

Immediately he found fresh sign—a single horse and rider had been through here after last night's storm. The marks were so fresh that Jim Branch actually pulled rein and dropped a hand to revolver-butt as he looked uneasily around him. But of course that was foolish; the sign was at least a few hours old. The horseman knew where he was going, and seemed unconcerned about anyone on his trail.

Jim Branch let the trapped wind out of his lungs, and left the gun in its holster. He touched steel to the roan, and went ahead. Always, the print of that single ridden horse overlay the older sign. He was familiar enough with those prints, by now, that he thought he could pick them out anywhere he came across them.

Abruptly, without warning, the trail broke out of the timber and spilled down an open slant into a shallow cup of meadow; Branch pulled in and drew his gun as he studied what lay before him. There was an open-fronted lean-to built of jackpine poles, a corral holding a single horse. No other movement, no other living thing.

His eyes narrowed, thinking of the horseman he had followed here and wondering about a trap. But he couldn't see a likely place for an ambusher to take cover. Only the lean-to looked at all suspicious, and he could find nothing wrong there. Meanwhile the minutes were ticking away. With an impatient curse, Branch kicked the roan and rode warily forward under the gathering, greasy-looking cloud ceiling.

As he dropped down into the meadow, that other horse caught the roan's scent and tossed up its head and came over to the corral bars. Branch had his gun ready and was trying to watch every side of him. No, he finally decided, there was nobody in the lean-to—only some things that looked as though they could be supplies stacked beneath a tarp. But there were smells about this place—smells of blood, and burning. And then he came upon a butcher's tripod, put together from peeled jackpine poles, and the whole operation suddenly became clear.

THE PAXMAN FEUD

Yes, here was where the slaughtered beef had been hung and skinned out; here, the bloody tarpaulin where the quarters were taken down and flung. Yonder the entrails and hides had been burned, and that muddy patch—if he dug into it—would probably yield the charred remains. He turned to the lean-to, actually thinking to look for a spade, when he saw something that made that unnecessary.

A red-and-white cowhide lay crumpled in the mud. Jim Branch quieted his horse, which didn't at all like this place, and swinging down shook out the stiff and bulky hide. He knew before he saw the brand that it would be Caufield's Seven Cross.

Needing a different taste in his throat, Branch took out a cigar and fired it up while he considered. He would like to know how long, and how often, Vern Paxman's crew had been bringing Caufield beef up here in small numbers and butchering them. And what happened to them afterward? This was one question, at least, that he meant to answer. But first the cowhide being too bulky a piece of evidence, he took out his knife and sawed away the section that contained Caufield's mark. The hide was fresh enough to be pliable; he folded the brand so he could stow it in a pocket of his coat. Then, to satisfy his curiosity on one further point, he walked over to the corral.

The horse—a spotted gray—was one of Paxman's Tomahawk string; its saddle was racked on the corral's top bar. The gray started to move away as Branch slid between the poles, then nervously stood its ground watching his approach. He got the halter, held it while he tapped the right foreleg. When, after a moment, the gray lifted its leg, he took the hoof in his hand and examined the shoe.

There was a bent frog that told him what he wanted to know. This was the horse that had led him up here.

As for the whereabouts of the rider, he could see the tracks of a wagon that led north across the meadow toward a break in the opposite timber. The impressions were recent but they followed ruts cut deep through earlier use. So this, too, was part of the routine; and Jim Branch, having learned all that this particular place could tell him, was already heading back to his ground-anchored roan, taking the reins and lifting to the saddle.

The trail was clearly marked, and, with a load of butchered meat aboard, the rig could hardly make much speed. He knew time was on his side and he rode without haste as he put his rented horse into those wagon ruts that led into the timber.

XI

THE DISTANT, carrying sound of an engine's whistle, drifting to him across the rock slants and surrounding stands of pine, lifted Jim Branch's head to listen and, for a moment, tightened his hand on the leather, bringing the roan to a stand. A look of bleak satisfaction etched itself into the tight set of his mouth as he nodded, grimly satisfied.

More and more, he had grown convinced that he knew where these wagon tracks were leading. When they took him through a low pass in the hill range he had been almost certain. When the tracks —by this time, a very fair wagon trace—debouched at last into a well-traveled road running along the western flank of the hills, he no longer had any doubt.

There could be but one destination for that load of fresh-butchered beef.

The engine sounded again, and, almost as at a

signal, the road bent and the ridges pulled back and perhaps a mile ahead he saw the tents and shacks and beehive activity of the construction camp. Southward the railroad spur ran back to join the main line out of Latigo; a little distance north of camp it ended abruptly on the raw, freshly graded embankment where even now crews were laboring to set the ties and push the steel forward. Jim Branch could see men toiling like ants, and the work engine sending up its streamers of pure white steam against the dirty cloud ceiling. The sound of the whistle came a little afterward, and was battered away to echoes against the flanks of the hills.

The camp itself seemed hardly smaller than Floyd Paxman's town on Sharp's Creek. Piles of tarp-covered supplies ranged alongside wooden-walled tents, forming a street where the wagon tracks he had been following were lost in the pattern of busy traffic. Branch rode in, trying to stay out of the way of the stream of men and mules and wagons, while he kept a careful lookout for anything that could be meaningful. And then he saw what he wanted—the mess tent, a big one, standing out against the orderly hubbub of the place. He reined his horse in that direction.

Through the front flaps he could see rows of long, oilcloth-covered wooden tables set with tinware, cups turned upside down on top of the plates. At the back, beyond a partition, was the whirling steam and clatter of the kitchen crew. Not pausing, Jim Branch rode on around toward the rear.

At once, he saw it: a wagon and team, backed close to the kitchen entrance. The mules were snuffling with their noses in feedbags. Dingy canvas had been rolled back and the tailgate lowered, and a couple of kitchen helpers were even now in the process of unloading stiff sides of beef and shouldering them inside the tent.

Branch rode alertly forward. He saw no one on the wagon's seat, no one in the vicinity he thought might be the driver. Letters were stenciled on the rolled-back canvas; he had to rein close and pull back one of the stiff folds before he could make out what the letters spelled: *F. PAXMAN*.

A voice shouted: "You! Get away from there! What do you think you're doing?"

Quickly he turned in saddle, right hand dropping in the vicinity of his holstered gun. The man who yelled at him had just ducked out under the flap of the kitchen tent and now stood arms akimbo—a big fellow, wearing the sleeves of dirty long johns whacked off high above his elbows, and a cook's apron tied about his middle.

Jim Branch kneed the roan and brought him to a stand in front of the cook. He said, "I'm looking for the fellow who drove this wagon here."

"What do you want with him?"

"My business."

The cook thought that answer over, decided he didn't like it. Brows like thorny bushes drew down, all but hiding his piggish eyes. He said gruffly, "Go on, you—beat it!"

Branch stiffened. He indicated the men who were removing the last sides of meat from the wagon. "I wonder if you realize it's stolen beef you're handling?"

"That's a lie!"

"I can prove it. Understand, I don't necessarily

accuse you of anything," he went on, as the other's look turned thunderous. "I wouldn't know what kind of arrangement you've got. But there's crooked work going on, just the same."

Something in his certainty seemed to turn the man cautious. He swallowed whatever angry words he had been about to say; scowling, he told Branch, "I make no arrangements. That's the commissary agent's job. I just take the supplies as they come."

"And, this commissary agent? Where do I find him?"

"Ward Oliver? That'd be hard to say. He don't come around much. I haven't seen him in over a week."

Branch rubbed the knuckles of a thumb across his jaw as he considered. From the kitchen came warm and interesting smells of food being prepared; they reminded him that it was long past noon, and a good many hours since the unsatisfactory breakfast he'd had at the town eat shack. Out on the right of way they were blasting rock. A rumble of black powder exploding rolled through the ground, shook the tent and made the roan move uneasily.

Branch said, "How often you get deliveries like this?"

"Couple times a week. Takes a lot of red meat to feed a crew of gandy dancers. But if there's anything crooked about the deal, *I* don't know it," the cook insisted belligerently. "The man brings it—I sign his book."

"Same man every time?"

"Not always. Usually he's a fellow about your size, yellow hair, sort of a squint to one eye. I never heard his name.

Neither had Jim Branch, but he knew the man. He nodded, recognizing the plain description of one of the three he'd seen moving stolen Seven Cross beef, in the hills day before yesterday.

The cook continued: "But today the driver's a new one to me. You give him a few minutes, he'll be coming back to pick up his wagon. In fact—" The man's eyes moved past his questioner; he motioned with his head. "There he is now...."

Branch turned quickly. Perhaps it shouldn't have surprised him, but somehow it hadn't occurred to him the driver of the wagon would be Hamp Billis. His jaw settled; deliberately he swung down, dropping the reins. The cook watched without expression as Branch walked over to the wagon.

It had now been unloaded, and Billis was at work lifting and fastening the tailgate, folding the canvas back to lash it in place. He was going forward to remove the feedbags from his mules when he heard someone behind him and looked around. Billis stood like that, frozen, his head twisted back across his shoulder. His face showed utter astonishment and, as he saw what was in Branch's expression, a beginning of fear. Suddenly he whipped about and backed away a step, until the shoulder of the near mule stopped him.

Jim Branch came to a stand, confronting him. He said coldly: "Hello, Billis. I thought Floyd Paxman gave you orders, yesterday, you were to make yourself scarce...."

The man's chest swelled. His sunburnt face turned even redder. "We ain't in Holster Basin now," he pointed out, hoarsely. "Anyhow, no man has the right to give an order like that. You can both go to hell!"

The attempt at bluster simply slid off its target. Branch never changed expression. "Does Floyd know about you hauling stolen beef in one of his wagons? Or, is the wagon stolen too?"

The breath exploded between the man's jaws. Suddenly the man's right arm was rising, clubbed fist reaching for his tormentor's face. Branch saw it coming and took the blow on a lifted forearm. The fist, scarred and toughened from handling the reins, was like an oak chunk and it had all Billis' fury and the weight of a muscular shoulder behind it; it numbed the bigger man's arm to the elbow as he blocked it. It also stung Jim Branch to real anger, and unleashed his own right fist in a hard, chopping blow that smashed directly against Billis' exposed jaw.

He heard teeth click together. Billis was flung, hard, against the flank of the mule behind him; when the animal tossed its head and stepped away, shouldering its mate, the man was dropped sprawling into the mud.

He was stunned, perhaps, but not unconscious. On his back, he lifted a hand feebly as Jim Branch stepped forward and leaned over him. Branch pulled open the man's coat, thinking there might be a gun under it. Billis, it seemed, was unarmed; but then something he saw half fallen from one of the coat pockets caught Branch's eye and, curious, he stooped for it. It was a business record book of some sort; he flipped it open, had a glimpse of columns of figures and dates and signatures.

A hand descended on his shoulder and he was hauled bodily around to look into the furious, scowling face of the tough cook. Next instant the face, and everything else, was blotted from sight by the massive fist that came over and exploded full in his face. His legs seemed to dissolve. The ground leaped up and struck his shoulders and the back of his head, and fireworks went off all over the place.

The mud was cold, and the chill of it seemed to work itself into his clothing; yet he was sure he couldn't have been lying there very long. When he opened his eyes he saw everything much as it had been when he went down—the high bulk of the mess tent against gray clouds, the wagon and team standing close by with the mules still snuffling into their feed bags. Branch placed a palm against the chill mud and pushed himself up to a sit. He could taste blood and when he touched a hand to his face it felt swollen and raw where the cook's fist had smashed him. He swore, and looked at the men who stood about, staring at him. The kitchen crew, he thought. And the big cook, himself, a mean and belligerent gleam in his piggish little eyes.

Jim Branch turned his head, searching for Hamp Billis; the man was gone. That jarred him and brought him up to one knee, where he paused on his way to his feet long enough to let the world ease off a momentary spinning. He lifted his head, sought out the tough cook. "All right! Where did he go?"

"You don't have to know," the cook told him gruffly. "He's gone. You've roughed him up as much as you're going to."

Branch felt his temper slipping. "You dumb bastard! I tell you, I had him dead to rights. That beef that he delivered, and you signed for, was stolen."

The big fellow wagged his massive head. Doggedly he said, "I know nothing at all about that. All I seen was one guy beating up on another one. Could both of you be crooks, for all of me."

Jim Branch swore at him again, and then impatience hauled him to his feet. His hat had dropped from his head when he went down. He scooped it up, and saw the book he'd taken from Billis, also lying in the mud. He got that and slipped it into a pocket, dragged on the hat. His gun was still in the holster. He laid a hand on the butt of it as he told the tough cook, "I've had about all the trouble I'm going to take. I want no more from you!"

Neither the cook nor his friends made answer. They stood, silent and unmoving, as Jim Branch walked over to his horse and pulled himself into the saddle. "You're going to have to take care of the wagon," he said, "until somebody comes to claim it." He turned his back on them, then, still shaking off that crusher to the jaw as he set out to search the construction camp for Hamp Billis.

The man had purely vanished, whether he'd allowed the camp to swallow him up or had managed to escape—perhaps on a horse he had promoted somehow; even perhaps afoot, to hide out in the timber somewhere until Branch gave up hunting. He had what he needed, anyway—the evidence of what he had seen today, backed by the book in his pocket and the brand cut from a Seven Cross steer hide. Jim Branch called off his search. No going near the mess tent again—there was probably nothing more to be got out of the cook—he put the roan once more on the trail, which would take him across the hills again, to Holster Basin.

It was well past midafternoon, by now, the sun angling toward still further ridges in the west; it would be dark before he reached the Basin. Knowing no better route than the one that had brought him over, Branch stuck to that. Where the less-traveled pass trail cut away from the main south road, he turned with it into a draw that pointed toward the barrier rising before him. Soon the timber closed in and he was climbing steadily. . . .

There was no warning at all when the rifle bullet struck a boulder with a stinging whine; a split instant later the report of the weapon itself went battering off through the hills, in receding waves. Jim Branch, with the quickness of instinct, had given a yank of the reins that pulled his horse into the protection of a rock face. Bent forward slightly beneath the overhang, he studied his immediate surroundings, and waited for a repetition of the shot.

Moments passed. His eyes searched and found where that bullet had hit—a clean, glancing streak across the top of the boulder. His eyes narrowed as he considered the angle of fire, the possible distance. The would-be ambusher had to be somewhere above and behind him.

Quickly he slid from saddle, fastening the reins to a tough-rooted bush. Afterward, drawing his gun and hugging cover, he turned back looking for a place where he believed he could climb. A washout, some time in the past, had eaten out a shallow trough. Cautiously he eased into it; loose rubble and sliding dirt made it difficult to negotiate, but he sought the aid of brush and any solid handhold and wormed his way upward, careful not to disturb the brush covering the slope. The kicking of his boots started small landslides, and loose dirt worked its way under his collar and into the sleeves of his coat. He couldn't know but what, at any moment, another rifle bullet would come tearing into that scrub, targeting his movements.

Then he crawled around a hump of rock and, suddenly, past thin screen of wiry brush, he saw his man some dozen yards above and ahead of him. It was Hamp Billis, standing at a crouch, in his hands the rifle with which he was evidently hoping for another shot. A horse was tied to a stunted tree a little distance away.

Jim Branch felt the hard settling of his jaw. There was no one worse in his book than an ambusher, and it added just one more item to the count against this man. He braced boots and knees to hold his position in that precarious slanting trough; and while one hand gently eased aside a branch of spiny manzanita, the other raised the barrel of the Colt. His sights settled on that halfbent figure. It was a fair distance for a hand gun, but he had a clean and easy target; the temptation was strong to take it, and be rid of Billis for good. But something held him.

As he hesitated, it was almost as though some uncharted sense spoke a warning to the man under his gun. Billis jerked his head up and around; his whole body swung, the rifle swept in a searching arc. For an instant it seemed to point directly at the spot where Jim Branch crouched in hiding.

The rifle dropped to arm's length. Hamp Billis ran the palm of a hand across his face. He looked again in the direction where he had thrown off his bullet. Abruptly he turned, and started for his horse.

Branch had had every chance he needed to shoot him, and yet had held off the trigger. Now, as Billis started to move away, the Colt's sights swung with him a moment before Jim Branch shook his head, and lowered the weapon. He said aloud, "Let him go!"

His natural repugnance against shooting an unsuspecting victim was reinforced by a sudden decision. He thought, *I'll let Billis carry his warning, and tell his boss what happened at the railroad camp!* True, it would increase Jim Branch's personal danger; but it could also bring things to a head. And he was of a mood to welcome that!

He waited until the sound of the other horse had faded out to nothing, and Hamp Billis was clearly gone. Putting away his gun, then, he proceeded to work back down the trough, in a slide of dirt and loose gravel, to the place where the roan waited.

XII

DUSK WAS THICKENING before Branch had managed to work his way down from the hills; by the time he reached the Basin's floor, full dark had arrived. A rising moon, just clearing the timbered eastern wall, was spreading silver across the sky—the clouds had broken at last and pulled back as day was ending.

Jim Branch, with a weary horse under him, was anxious now to get on to town as quickly as he could; matters there, he thought, were almost certain to come to a head before the night was finished. But the thought was jarred from him suddenly as he came out of the timber and saw, winking at him across the distance, something that looked bright enough to be a star fallen to the earth. Puzzled, he drew rein to study it.

It was much too bright to be the lamplit window of a ranchhouse; besides, it was too unsteady—seeming to fade and spring brighter again, as a star does. Jim Branch scowled thoughtfully, running a palm across his cheek that was tender where the tough cook had smashed him. Suddenly he swore as an explanation occurred to him, one he knew he couldn't afford to ignore. He shook his head, pulled the reluctant horse around and used the spurs to send it up the Basin floor, almost directly opposite from the way he wanted to go.

The moon brightened, and presently he struck the main wagon road and the going was easier. He hit the creek at a shallow fording and took it without slackening pace—bottom stones rattling, moonglow turning the water to lace as the roan's hooves churned it up. By this time he'd lost the spot of brightness which had alarmed him, but presently the ground lifted slightly and he saw it again—

Another mile, and now he thought he could see the whipping of flames and the stream of sparks. When he came to a fence and halted to lean from saddle and work with the loop of wire that held the gate, he was positive that the sound the night wind brought him was a sporadic, angry popping of gunfire.

He booted the roan ruthlessly. Minutes later the flat ground dipped away and there ahead were a half dozen stacks of cut hay neatly ranked, all burning. Fire made a crackling roar, and the cold wind that pressed in whipped the separate tongues of flame and sent streamers of sparks curling skyward. Aided by the moonglow, the fitful light gave almost an illusory imitation of midday.

He drew rein. The guns were silent for the moment at least. Over to his right, just beyond the fireglow's edge, he caught a movement and made out what appeared to be the shapes of men and horses. He drew his gun as a precaution, and directed a shout that way: "Caufield?"

The answer came back, a doubtful challenge: "Who's there?"

Instead of answering, Branch kicked the roan and headed him toward the voice. Doing so, he felt the heat of the closest fire touch him briefly and in that instant there was the flashing report of a rifle somewhere; a second one echoed it. But if they were meant for him, both shots missed. After that, Branch was out of the light and into the shadows beyond.

As he blinked to clear the smeared image of the fires from his vision, armed and mounted figures were suddenly closing in around him. Wes Caufield exclaimed, "Branch! Is that you?"

The roan shied nervously as the other horses crowded it. He settled it before he spoke. "So, they decided to use a torch on your feed. . . ."

"Yeah." Caufield's voice was bitter and angry. "And now there's a dozen rifles up on that rim to your left, determined to keep us from doing anything to put it out. They came mighty near tagging you!"

Branch's night vision was working again. He saw young Caufield and a couple other riders that he judged were what remained of his Seven Cross crew. A little distance away someone was laying motionless on the ground. "They get one of you?" Jim Branch demanded.

"It's Fargo," Wes told him. "He took a bullet, first thing when we saw the fires and came hurrying to see what was wrong...."

Margie Caufield knelt beside the injured ranch cook. She was dressed like the men, in shirt and jeans and a wide-brimmed range hat; as she stood and came to join them, her identity was betrayed by the smallness of her figure, the contour of her silhouette against the background of burning stacks. She carried a carbine by the balance, but like the men she seemed baffled, helpless to use it.

"How do I get up on that rim?" Branch demanded.

"You mustn't try it!" the girl answered him quickly. "There's too many of them."

Her brother said, "There's a break, a hundred yards or so to the west. But, she's right. Even if a man could make it up there—"

Jim Branch wasn't listening. He was still enough of a cattleman, himself, that this willful, wanton destruction of previous winter feed tripped an angry trigger in him. He leaned in the saddle, and before Margie Caufield could protest, he reached down and took the carbine from her hands. "I'm borrowing this, if you don't mind!" And, not waiting for comment, he jerked the roan around and fed it the steel.

He swung wide, keeping in the darkness this time. He had ridden only a little way when he heard another horse behind him and, looking about, saw Wes Caufield spurring hard after. "If you're crazy enough to try it," the young fellow said, "I guess I'm crazy enough to back you up." The rifle barrel in his hand winked a flash of moonlight as he swung it, pointing. "Bear a little more to your left."

THE PAXMAN FEUD

The rim was shallow, a line of caprock cresting a rise of perhaps a hundred feet. Branch saw the break Caufield had spoken of, and pointed for it. The ground began to lift, flinty and studded by scrubby sagebrush growth. Then this growth ended and the horse was fighting the drag of loose soil.

A whack on the rump with the flat of the carbine urged it on; a prodigious lunge of his shoulder muscles, and it dug in and the jagged edges of broken rimrock slid past. With Wes Caufield's horse somewhere behind and below him, Jim Branch topped out on the very edge of the rim—just in time to meet a lash of flame from a rifle muzzle.

He had remembered to work the carbine's lever, making sure there was a cartridge under the firing pin. Now as the frightened roan squealed and tried to rear, he threw off a hasty shot. Fighting his mount, he flipped the weapon one-handed, working the lever, and clamped the butt beneath his elbow for a second try.

The rifle let go again, with no better results. For, just then, something barreled into Jim Branch from the rear, nearly throwing the roan completely off its feet—Wes Caufield, too eager, had failed to check his mount as he came charging up through the break in the rimrock. By the time they broke the tangle and Branch had the roan under control so he could look around again, it was to discover the rifleman was gone.

Puzzled, he started along the edge of the rim hunting a target. Down below the stacks were still burning, like a half dozen separate torches, but by now he suspected there was little left to burn—the raiders had been too effective in holding Seven

Cross at bay and preventing them from combating the windwhipped flames. His jaw was set hard as he rode ahead, scarcely noting whether Caufield was behind him or not.

A little back from the rim, suddenly, he heard an uneasy stirring of horses and a creaking of leather —the unmistakable sounds of men hurriedly mounting their saddles. He thought he saw them against a denser blackness of scrub cedar and rock. And, drawing in, he stood in the stirrups and whipped the carbine's stock to his cheek, angrily shot and levered and shot again into that tangle of men and horses.

He heard curses, a yelp of pain; a sixgun blasted purple fire but the bullet came nowhere close. Then the firing pin slapped harmlessly on an empty chamber, and he realized he'd cranked the carbine dry. Almost without thinking he dropped the weapon and had grabbed out his sixshooter, before cold reason returned to tell him it was foolishness, charging a body of armed men with nothing but the five shells in the cylinder of a Colt revolver.

Even as he hesitated, the racket of a bunch of horses being plunged into a gallop suddenly filled the night, and as quickly faded. Within moments all sound of them had died; there was only the rattle of the night wind in dry cedars along the rim. Jim Branch drew a long breath and shoved his sixgun, unfired, back into the holster.

He had just stepped down to retrieve the empty carbine when Wes Caufield came riding out of the darkness. Branch responded to his cautious hail and rode to meet him. "You all right?"

"Me?" Caufield uttered an angry grunt. "I wasn't in on any of it! You drove them off, single-handed."

"Nobody drove them off," Branch said. "I think they were ready to leave. Those fires have just about burned themselves out."

A look over the rim confirmed it. Now that the enemy had gone, Caufield's two cowhands could be seen hastily pulling what was left of the stacks apart, trying to scatter the fire and save as much as they could.

Caufield said heavily, "Nothing more to do up here...."

They let the horses take their time, picking a way down again. When they had negotiated it and were able to talk as they rode, Jim Branch asked Caufield, "Did you see or hear anything in all this that would definitely identify them?"

"I saw one fellow, for about a half a second, who certainly looked a lot like Nick Roddy. But no, I couldn't take it into a court."

But Branch was willing to believe it. He remembered Roddy's disappointment over not being allowed to finish burning out Floyd Paxman's store and possibly the whole town of Sharp's Creek; he could well believe Roddy might have been handed this assignment tonight just to placate him, and give him a chance to put the torch to something.

Margie Caufield was waiting anxiously for their return; Jim Branch handed her back the empty carbine he had borrowed and, as Wes answered his sister's questions, dismounted and walked over for a look at the wounded cook.

Fargo was conscious, and short of temper; he sat

with his back against a stump, nursing the bullet-gouged forearm for which Margie had fashioned a makeshift bandage. His eyes glittered with suspicion. "*You* again!" he muttered. "Why the hell do you keep showing up? Are you Tomahawk or ain't you?"

Amused, Branch said without answering his question, "I'm glad to see you're at least feeling good enough to make you mean."

The cook growled at him, and Branch turned and walked back to the Caufields.

He could hear Wes Caufield talking to his sister in a tone of utter discouragement—and this was alarming, for in their short acquaintance Branch had come to think of the fellow as a scrapper, not easily put off by the odds against him. But now he said, heavily, "I wonder why we don't admit we're licked!"

"Licked?" Margie couldn't seem to believe her ears. "Because of this? Why, all they did was burn some hay. And only the first cutting, at that. There'll be more."

"Sure!" he echoed in the same tone. "More for them to burn whenever they feel like it. And what about the boys? After what just happened to Fargo, how can I ask them to go on fighting this thing?"

"Then you've decided to quit?" Jim Branch challenged as he walked up. He spoke calmly enough, but the barb in his words brought Wes swinging around to face him. The angry reaction told him what he needed to know, and he added, "You don't really mean it. I don't believe so, and neither does Margie. Not as long as there's a chance for a break."

Wes Caufield was peering at him narrowly. He had been stung, which was what Branch had wanted; now he threw a savage challenge of his own: "I'm paying you plenty to find me that break, Mister Branch. Suppose you earn your pay!"

"Wes!" Margie protested—completely surprising Jim Branch, to hear her defend him. "Be fair! He's only been here two days!"

Branch hoped she read the thanks in the nod he gave her. He said, "The fight is a long way from lost. As it happens I'm working on something right now; but you have to give me a little time." It was as close as he meant to come, telling them what he had learned in the hills and what he still expected to accomplish tonight.

The young fellow appeared chastened. His whole manner had changed as he answered, "Sure, Jim. I'm sorry. You're only one man, and I don't hope for miracles." He swallowed. "Though, maybe a miracle is what it's going to take!"

All at once his voice was shaking with emotion. Abruptly he turned, flung himself into the saddle, and rode to join his punchers who were still trying to put out the fires.

Looking after him, Margie spoke in a troubled voice. "I don't know what to say to him. He's really desperate. I've never seen him quite like this before. I don't know what he'll do. . . ."

"Keep an eye on him," Branch told her. "But let him alone. We all get discouraged—and we just have to work it out."

"Of course, you're right. But —I feel so useless!" He heard her sigh, felt her shoulder brush his arm as she turned away.

She was probably no less discouraged than her brother, if the truth were told; knowing what he did of her, he could imagine what her reaction must have been to this scene of destruction and blazing guns.

She was too much concerned about Wes to let her own feelings show. He said, gently, "Not useless. Here's Fargo needing you, for one. I hope the old boy isn't too badly hurt."

"Oh, no." She shook the tiredness from her voice. "He'll be fine, I'm sure, once we get him to the ranch and make him comfortable." She looked at him. "You'll be coming with us, of course?"

Branch hesitated. It was an invitation he'd have liked to accept. For one thing, he had eaten nothing since morning and he had a vivid memory of that one meal the girl had fixed for him. But there was a gnawing impatience in him that drew him on to Sharp's Creek, and so he shook his head. "Thanks. I think I'd better be getting back to town."

He was already turning to the roan, checking the cinch before he sought stirrup and swung astride.

Yonder, the fires had finally burnt themselves out; they could hear the men's voices now, as they came leading their mounts. On some impulse Margie Caufield stepped closer to Branch's horse and placed a hand upon the saddle fender. He saw her face, pale in the moonglow, as she said, "You'll be careful?" And suddenly he knew that, somehow, she'd guessed he wasn't telling everything he could.

The sincere concern in her words touched him. For a moment he could only sit with the reins in his hand, looking down at the pale disk of her face.

"Why, sure—always!" he said and with a gruff "Good night," pulled away. But as he rode away, hunting again the wagon ruts that could point him in the direction of the town, his thoughts were full of her—and of how things might have been if she had not been a girl who feared and hated gunmen.

If he might have been someone with a different past, or even some promise of a future.

XIII

THE TOWN, a huddle of buildings among the half-cut timber along the creekbank, seemed completely quiet tonight; the lamps that glowed in occasional windows were fainter than the spread of light from the moon, high amid the tattered remnants of the day's cloud ceiling. A couple of saddled horses were tied to the big pine near the lighted saloon. Too dark under there to make out the brands they wore, if any, but Jim Branch made a mental checkmark against them.

A lantern was burning on a roofprop inside the livery barn. Ed Troy failed to appear when he rode up the ramp and dismounted, so Branch stripped the saddle, hung up the sweaty blanket, and put the tired roan into a stall. He got grain for it from the feed bin, and then set about rubbing it down with an old sack he found. If the roan had been getting fat from need of exercise, he had more than given it a workout today.

In this stillness the pleasant music of the creek dominated other sounds, and so he failed completely to hear anyone enter the barn. He was surprised, therefore, to discover Floyd Paxman watching him, hands thrust deep into the pockets of the rumpled suit, a scowl on the gaunt features. Branch gave him a nod. "Good evening."

Paxman returned neither nod nor greeting. He said without preliminary, "I saw you ride in. Just where the hell have you been all day?"

Branch tossed aside the sack he'd been using, came out of the stall and closed and fastened the half-door. Looking squarely at Floyd, he said briefly, "I took a little ride."

"On my time?" the freighter exclaimed. "Damn it, supposing I had needed you?"

"I didn't think it was likely," Branch replied coolly. "Not after the resistance Tomahawk met here yesterday. They weren't apt to make a try any time soon at burning the town. Meanwhile I had something I wanted to check on. I think it should more than interest you."

He had taken from his coat pocket a ragged section cut out of a steer hide, bearing the scabbed brand mark of Wes Caufield's Seven Cross. Floyd Paxman turned it over in his hands. "What's this?"

"Together with this," Jim Branch said, as he handed over the book he'd taken off Hamp Billis, "it's evidence." Paxman looked at the cover, which was stamped with the name of his own freighting firm. Opening it he thumbed through the pages, a businessman's practiced eye quickly scanning colums of figures and dates and signatures. He lifted his stare to Jim Branch.

"Suppose you tell me where you got this. And what it's all about...."

"Those are the receipts for the delivery of dressed beef—and that's the brand off one of the carcasses." Briefly as he could he told of what he'd learned from the tough cook at the construction camp, of the attempt by Hamp Billis to lay an ambush for him. In conclusion he admitted, "I don't know all the details yet. For example, whether the railroad's commissary man is taking a cut of the profits on this stolen meat, or if the deal was made in good faith where he was concerned."

Floyd Paxman's eyes stabbed him. "But there's no question in your mind that my brother Vern is behind it?"

"Looks plain enough to me. His crew runs off Seven Cross stock and does the butchering. They've got hold of at least one of your wagons, and they make the deliveries in your name. When Hamp Billis had to report we'd unmasked him and his value as a spy was ended, Vern sent him to do the driving chores which were more down his alley.

"They may even have other markets besides the railroad—the signed receipts in the book ought to tell. In any case, it's all a part of the scheme to break Wes Caufield—and you've been made the goat. You could go to the sheriff, or to a U.S. marshal, with this evidence."

"Yes," Floyd Paxman said, nodding. The word came out in a long, sibilant sigh. "You could...." He straightened then, his gaunt head lifting, his mouth a hard line. "All right, Branch. I take it back. You're a smart fellow, all right. You used your head—and what you've just turned up could blow things wide open.... Come along," he said abruptly, and, turning, started for the door with a purposeful stride. Jim Branch, wondering how much longer he would have to wait for a chance to put something in his empty belly, followed more deliberately.

As they stepped into the street, Floyd appeared to stumble. For an instant he shouldered into Branch, throwing him briefly offstride. Even as it occurred to Branch what was happening, he heard the scrape of bootleather, and something that could only be a sixgun's muzzle was suddenly rammed into his ribs. Another voice murmured, "Easy, now! Don't be a fool—you've made enough mistakes for one day!"

It had been neatly done, Floyd crowding him just enough so he couldn't make a play for his Colt even if he'd wanted to. It made his blunder all the more unforgivable; after all, he'd known he was walking into treachery but had been confident he could handle it when it showed. Silently cursing his faulty reactions, he felt the slight tug at his belt as the gun was lifted from its holster. Now Vern Paxman stepped around into sight, holding both is own weapon and the one he'd taken off the prisoner.

The brothers stood looking at him. Floyd said, in a voice that shook a little with tension, "Can't be too careful. Killer like him could have another gun on him somewhere."

"Search him, then," Vern ordered curtly.

Floyd made clumsy work of it by the lantern light from inside the barn. The only thing he found in the nature of a weapon was Branch's pocket knife, and he helped himself to that. Then he stepped back, saying, "He's clean, I guess."

Vern wagged his big head. "Good!" He shoved the captured gun away behind his belt. His blocky face was sinister in the half light as he told Branch: "And you'd best stay careful, because I'm taking no chances with you. Now, walk!"

"Where?"

"Where I tell you!"

He cuffed the prisoner's shoulder, turning him with force enough almost to fling him to his knees. When the two brothers fell in at either side he found they were pointing him in the direction of the bar, which was surprising—he would have thought they'd take him to the privacy of Floyd's office in the store building. But he offered no argument.

They moved through frosty moonlight and inky shadows, their boots making a ragged rhythm. Somewhere in the village, a dog barked a few times and was silent. Branch could hear the creek pouring through its channel nearby. And the rumble of his own empty belly.

The emptiness inside him was only partly hunger, now. Even stronger was the sick, hollow ache of mortal fear. That he had deliberately walked into this made it no more pleasant. . . .

The horses tied under the big pine stirred at their tethers; they were the only living things on the street. They tramped up the steps of the saloon and Vern reached around Branch to turn the knob and shove the door open. Inside, the bar had a dingy look, poorly lighted by a single lamp burning in a wall bracket. At a table beneath it, with a bottle and glasses in front of them, sat Hamp Billis and a yellowhaired puncher with a curiously drooping eyelid. There was no sign of Durkin, the bartender. Probably he'd been ordered again to make himself scarce.

The moment his eye lit on Branch, the yellowhaired man was surging to his feet. He told Vern, "That's him, boss. That's the guy, all right."

Vern Paxman kicked the door shut. "Of course he's the one," the Tomahawk owner said roughly. "Nick Roddy was a fool to let him see you moving steers—it came within an ace of causing more trouble than anyone could handle. Well," he added, "luckily there's no harm done. For which we can thank Billis, using his head today, and getting word back to us as quick as he did."

At the praise, Hamp Billis positively smirked with pleasure.

Vern stepped around Branch, to resume the chair he had evidently left when he went out to the barn. He had left a cigar resting on the table's edge; he picked it up, put it in his mouth and tongued it into a corner. He looked at the prisoner. "Sit down."

Not speaking, Branch stepped forward and eased into the only empty chair, with Billis at his right. The muleskinner moved slightly in his place, drawing away from him. The puncher with the drooping lid had already resumed his seat, and now Floyd Paxman hauled up a chair from another table and folded his gaunt length onto it, between his brother and Jim Branch.

Vern indicated the whisky bottle. "Pass me that, Sid." The yellowhaired man handed it over and the rancher poured himself a drink. He swallowed about half, then put the cigar back into his mouth, but now he found the cigar had gone out and he dug up a match, which he scratched alight on the underside of the table.

As he puffed the smoke to life, he considered Jim Branch coldly above his cupped hands. "Now the problem is—what do we do with you?"

"I can see my being around can be embarrassing," Branch admitted, refusing to give these men any satisfaction by letting even a hint of fear into his voice. "For everybody," he added, and looked deliberately at Floyd. It was the freighter who broke gaze and let his own stare slide away. Branch said, "I know too much. And I can guess a little more."

"And just what do you know?" Vern Paxman demanded, his eyes on the prisoner's.

Jim Branch shrugged. "Why, for one thing, I know this supposed feud between the two of you over the future of Holster Basin is about ninety percent hogwash. It's obvious to me Floyd knew all the time his wagons were being used to haul stolen Caufield beef—likely he set it up with the railroad, himself. But I pretended to be fooled, just now, for the same reason I let Billis go when he tried to ambush me: I wanted matters brought to a head."

Vern looked at his brother. "And *this* is what you hired to try and use against me!"

The other's gaunt cheeks were tinged with angry color. "How was I to know this would happen? How'd I know he'd stick his nose in where it didn't belong?"

"You might at least have given it a thought!" his brother snapped. As Vern turned away, Floyd snatched up the whisky bottle; his hand trembled a little, pouring a drink which he tossed off with a convulsive shudder as though it were medicine.

Vern Paxman spoke again to the prisoner. "This is interesting. Let's hear some more."

Branch saw no reason why not. It might sound as though he were talking to buy himself a bullet, but he was due for one anyway; the longer he could keep them listening, the longer he would have to seek a break and a way out. And so he answered, though his own ears were aghast at the rashness of what he was saying, and he could feel the cold sweat trickling down his ribs.

"What's had me curious," he said, "is that your brother is more of a match for you than it might look. Here you've got a crew of men like Nick Roddy, while, until he hired me to bodyguard him, Floyd had no guns on his side at all—and yet, he's held you to a standstill. So far as I see, there's only one weapon he could be holding over you."

"And that would be?"

"His money. I'm only guessing, but I'm wondering if maybe he didn't put up the capital for your takeover of Tomahawk and Holster Basin. If he's holding your legal note, he'd be able to haul you into court to collect any time he wanted.

"Or—wait a minute!" Jim Branch snapped his fingers as a fresh thought struck him. "I'm still guessing; but why is it he's been going behind your back, trying to talk Wes Caufield into accepting a loan all the time he was supposed to be helping you to break him? Could it be that after you'd gone to all the trouble, he meant to be in a position to grab Seven Cross on Caufield's mortgage—and leave you out in the cold?"

Vern Paxman snatched the stub of cigar from his lips. His face was suddenly congested with angry color. And Branch knew he had hit upon the truth.

"Would you ever believe such gall?" the Tomahawk boss demanded. "He knows damn well how thin I'm spread—he knows I'm relying on what I get from Seven Cross to meet his note. If he can just take it himself, and then hit me with a court action—I'd be shut out completely! The whole Basin would be his. *That's* my dear brother for you!" Vern Paxman flung the cigar savagely to the floor, and there was pure hatred in the stare he turned on his kinsman. "By God, I should have gone ahead and let Nick Roddy kill him!"

Floyd had turned white and the bony hand that rested on the tabletop was visibly shaking. But he met his brother's stare.

"So I got a little greedy!" he exclaimed in a voice that was hoarse with strain. "Can't we forget that? It's no more than you'd have done, in my place. Right now, it's more important that this man can make bad trouble for us both, unless he's taken care of." His bitter eyes turned to Branch. His thin mouth pulled down hard. "I suppose it was blackmail you had in mind?"

Jim Branch was satisfied to let him think so. But Vern Paxman, anger toward his brother for the moment allayed, was studying the prisoner now and he slowly shook his head. "I don't think so, somehow." It was almost as though he were working it out as he spoke. "I don't think we know at all, yet, what he's doing here." He looked at Floyd. "You tell me you only hired him because you were scared after Roddy got drunk and went after Wes Caufield at the station in Latigo. But, if it's so—if you didn't bring him into this country—*what was Jim Branch doing on that train?*"

The room and the night seemed to hold their breaths as four pairs of eyes centered on the prisoner, waiting for an answer. And then the street door opened. Wes Caufield strode into the bar.

XIV

YOUNG CAUFIELD seemed not at all aware of what he had walked into. He scarcely glanced toward the five men seated around the table at the other side of the room; instead he went directly to the bar, and when he saw there was no one on duty he swore and rapped his knuckles sharply on the wood. "What is this?" he demanded loudly. "Can't a man buy himself a drink?"

It was then that Jim Branch realized the young fellow had already taken on a fair amount of liquor, somewhere between here and his moment of defeat in the burned-out stockyard. Branch suddenly remembered his dark despondency following the raid, and his sister saying hopelessly, *"He's desperate. I've never seen him quite like this before. I don't know what he might do...."*

Well, here he was, trying to do what many another impulsive man might in the face of continued frustration—let off tension, momentarily at least, with the help of whisky. Only, he apparently was having little success, because plainly he wasn't very drunk. When he swung away from the bar to face the room, his movements were sure; the lamp in the wall bracket showed his features only a shade heightened in their color. His glance, roving the room, located the five men seated about the round-topped table; it fell upon Vern Paxman's face, and stopped there. His whole body stiffened. "*You!*"

Vern Paxman had picked up his glass. Over the rim of it he said briefly, "I've got no time to bother with you. Get out!" And he drank.

What he saw in the younger man's face made Jim Branch lean forward lightly, tucking the toes of his boots behind the legs of his chair. The contemptuous dismissal had knotted Wes Caufield's rope-tough hands into fists.

"Damn you! You can break a man but you can't be bothered to look at him—is that what you're telling me?' Wes' voice rose a note. "You don't get rid of me that easy!"

Deliberately Vern Paxman set down his empty glass. He pushed back his chair and rose, without haste; he turned, his solid bulk looming above his challenger. "I'm looking at you," he said coldly. "If you've got anything worth my hearing, then get it said!"

Young Caufield took a step toward him, body bent slightly forward, one hand dropping dangerously close to the gun that was strapped to his hip. If he made the mistake of touching it, he was probably a dead man—a glance at the yellowhaired puncher, Sid, lifted the short hairs on the back of Jim Branch's neck; for he saw the menacing eye of a sixgun looking squarely at Wes just above the table's edge.

Caufield, unaware of anyone but the man who stood directly before him, was speaking in a voice that shook with anger. "How long do you mean to play cat and mouse with me? Damn you . . . I suppose you'll even deny it was you that had my feed yard burned out tonight?"

Paxman answered the charge calmly enough. "Why should I bother to deny it? That ranch of yours is nothing more than a nuisance. Sooner you realize it, the better."

That was more than Wes Caufield could take. Branch almost cried out a warning but it was already too late. Vern Paxman was prepared and his own gun cleared leather while the young fellow's hand was still reaching toward his holster. Vern did not fire; he didn't have to. His arm rose and made a chopping sweep. The hat was knocked from Caufield's head and as he stumbled back hard, against the edge of the bar, his own half-drawn weapon was jarred from his fingers and fell in a blur of lamplight on blued steel, to strike the brass bar rail a clanging blow.

Hanging there, braced on widespread boots, Wes Caufield looked down at the gun for a long, dazed moment. Slowly, then, he lifted his head. The front sight of Paxman's revolver had scored his forehead with a streak of red, and blood was running in a stream down one side of his face and dripping upon his shirt front. A dazed and humiliated man, he peered at his tormentor, and at Paxman's gun pointed at his chest.

Vern Paxman's voice dripped with cold contempt. "Want some more?"

Wes drew a shuddering breath. Still half blind with pain, his eyes moved on to the men still seated about the table, passed from face to face as though not really seeing them—until it came to rest, suddenly, on Jim Branch. An expression of puzzlement, quickly fading into something else, showed itself on Caufield's bleeding and tortured face. His mouth worked, seemingly unable to speak. The single word came out as a croak—and a plea for help: "*Jim—?*"

Branch slid his eyes away from Caufield's, looked across the table at Sid. The muzzle of the gun, just resting on the table's edge, had shifted and now was pointing squarely toward himself.

But Wes Caufield couldn't see the gun, or Jim Branch's empty holster. All he saw in his pain was a man he had relied on and who now sat with his enemies, not stirring and not offering to lift a hand in this moment when he stood in need of it. A raw and unreasoning emotion seemed to whip through him and leave him shaken; his hurt eyes blazed with outrage and despair. "Is that how it is, Jim?" he demanded hoarsely. "Are you selling me out? Have you really switched over to the other side?"

Jim Branch groaned inwardly, even as he realized young Caufield was too dazed to see what he was doing. From the subtle change in Vern Paxman's profile, he could guess that these few words had given the big man the answer to the last question that was puzzling him; Vern said, with a grunt of satisfaction, "So now we know! He was working for *you! You* brought him to Holster Basin—!"

Boots tramped the wooden steps outside the bar. The door was thrown open and Nick Roddy bulled his way in, and shouldered the door shut again. Roddy's voice, loud with satisfaction, boomed through the low-ceilinged room: "We done that job, chief. Believe me, we done it right! Wasn't a stack left standing in the yard when we—" He broke off in midstride, as he saw what he was interrupting. Briefly, every eye in that room had swung to him.

Jim Branch knew it was the only chance he would get. In the moment while attentions were taken, he was reaching to grab up the half-filled whisky bottle Floyd had set in front of him. He might have used it as a weapon; instead he flung the bottle directly at the lamp in its bracket on the wall facing him. The light was wiped away. As darkness descended he grasped the table's edge and tilted it to send it over against the yellowhaired man seated opposite. And without an instant's hesitation, Branch hurled himself after it.

He half expected to meet the blast of a gun in his face—could only hope he had managed somehow to trap and deflect it. One boot, lashing out to propel himself struck a yielding shape and he heard a grunt of pain, thought it must have been Hamp Billis who got in the way of the kick. The whole room was a bedlam of confused movement and yelling voices. And now Branch slammed all-out into his target and they both went down with Sid's chair toppling under them.

As they struck the floor Branch was groping desperately to locate that gun. By some miracle it hadn't gone off before. Now it did, so close to his ear he felt his skull had exploded with the concussion. But at least he knew now where the damn thing was; he chopped down with a forearm, was able to trap Sid's wrist against the floor.

The man under him was struggling and swearing. A fist struck him a glancing blow in the throat and slashed upward, almost taking his ear off. Gagging and choking on powdersmoke, Jim Branch hit back. He felt yielding flesh and gristle, and blood spurted hot and wet under his grinding fist. He must have smashed the man's nose.

Pain immobilized him, just long enough for Branch to shift and trap his gun wrist in a twisting grasp. He could hear Vern Paxman shouting to his men: "Sid! Nick!" Somewhere above him, a gun smashed two more shocks of sound into the confined space of the room's walls. Branch cringed from them, and slammed Sid's wrist against the floor and felt the fingers come open, lose their grip on the gunhandle. He freed the arm; missed the weapon, then found it and grabbed it up. He chopped down with the barrel and felt it land solidly against Sid's hard skull. The man quit struggling abruptly.

Rolling away and trying to get his knees under him, Branch became aware now of an eerie, flickering hint of light, where burning oil from the smashed lamp dripped down the wall to the floor. It was no more than a hint; while, across the room, the moonlight flooding the two front windows only made the darkness in this far corner seem all the more complete.

Once more, and not a half dozen feet from him, Vern Paxman's voice shouted: "Nick! You take Caufield. I'll get the other one. . . ." His voice was drowned in the mingled roar and flare of a pair of shots, the spears of flame crossing each other somewhere in the vicinity of the bar. Glass broke with a crash.

Branch collided with an empty chair and sent it clattering, and, just above him, a gun blasted at the sound. He thought he almost felt the heat of the muzzle flame, yet by some miracle the bullet failed to find him. It had been Vern Paxman's gun, he knew. As he wrenched himself to his feet and spun away, gripping the weapon he'd taken from Sid, he debated whether to risk a shot at the smeared afterimage.

The decision was never made. In the same instant a new weapon spoke, lighting that corner of the room with an instant's lurid, shuttering glare. Branch had a single glimpse of Vern Paxman staggering and already starting to fall. It remained printed on his vision after the darkness clamped down again—he was still seeing Vern's solid, sagging figure frozen grotesquely, even after Vern's body fell heavily against him on its way to the floor.

He staggered backward from the collision, reaching for balance. That probably saved his life, as the weapon that had killed Vern Paxman spoke again. Perhaps he made some dim sort of target, silhouetted against the streaks of dripping oil burning themselves out upon the wall behind him; he felt a blow along his ribs, but it only drove his shoulders against the wall and that steadied him enough to bring his gun level and work the trigger twice, punching a shot to either side of the flash of that other weapon.

A choked scream mingled with the collapse

across the overturned table; after that, suddenly, he was alone with the reek of cordite and burnt oil, and the dull throb of pain along his ribs.

And with the sound of an odd, muffled whimpering, which went on and on with hardly a stop for breath—the only thing that broke the quiet in the aftermath of the storm.

He touched a hand to his ribs, felt the warmth that soaked his shirt. No more than a shallow groove, he thought; he had certainly used up a big part of his quota of luck to have come through with no greater damage than this.

The darkness, and that crazy whimpering in a corner of the room, were beginning to get on his nerves. He remembered seeing another wall lamp, in the hallway no more than a few yards from where he stood; he went feeling his way along the wall in search of it.

He found the lamp and got it lit. Taking it down from its holder he carried it back into the bar, and looked about at the wreckage of the fight—carnage enough to sicken a man.

The bullet that killed Vern Paxman had taken him squarely in the face, and Branch quickly cut his eyes away from that sight. Floyd Paxman lay draped across the edge of the overturned table like a sack of empty clothes, his blood darkening the table's green baize. By the street door, Nick Roddy sprawled with arms and legs flung wide and his gun, still dribbling smoke, beside him. Sid was on the floor where Branch had put him with a blow from his own gunbarrel; he was alive, stirring a little now.

And pressed into a corner, Hamp Billis crouched

with his knees drawn up and his arms wrapped around them. The lamplight gleamed on his staring eyes, on his sweaty face. He was unhurt, but it was from his lips that the animal-like whimpering sounds were coming—as though from a man put clear out of his head by terror.

Jim Branch drew a long breath. He shoved the smoking gun into his holster and went to have an anxious look at Wes Caufield.

The young fellow lay against one end of the bar, a shoulder propped against it, head fallen upon his chest. Branch set the lamp on the floor and knelt. His face was bleak as he saw the blood on Caufield's clothing; but hasty examination showed that the boy had taken a bullet through the shoulder. He was alive and his wound far from fatal. And Jim Branch breathed easier—Wes was game, if young and maybe lacking sometimes in judgment. The years would give him that.

They did, or a man just didn't survive. But Branch had hope for Wes Caufield....

Excited voices, now, drawing nearer—a growing sound of boots on gravel, and then, after a moment's hesitation, coming up the steps. The door came open a few inches, until it met the obstacle of Nick Roddy's lifeless body. Branch called, "Push him out of the way." His voice was curt with the aftermath of what he had been through, and with the burn of his scored ribs. Those outside tried again, and Roddy's corpse gave enough to let them slip inside, one at a time.

Troy, the liveryman, was the first to enter, with Herb Mattox and other people of Sharp's Creek crowding behind him. They stopped dead, staring in horror at what they found. "My God!" Ed Troy cried shakily. "Did you do all this?"

"No." Branch felt he could use a drink. Straightening up carefully to favor that scored rib, he placed the lamp on the bar and went around behind it, broken glass crunching underfoot. He found a bottle that was intact, and a tumbler, and poured himself a shot. He felt better when it went down.

Only then did he answer their stammered questions. "Floyd Paxman killed his brother. Whether he did it deliberately, or trying to get at me, I guess we never will know. It was young Caufield did for Nick Roddy."

In spite of the whisky he suddenly felt unbearably weak. He set down his glass and took hold of the edge of the counter, trying to steady himself. "I've heard that you know about gunshot wounds. Caufield's the one who needs attention. The rest—"

The Paxmans and Nick Roddy were beyond help, he was thinking; Sid would probably be recovering from that stunning blow with the gun-barrel. Hamp Billis hadn't even been touched.

But the chilling sound of that demented, meaningless whimpering coming from the man crouched in the corner was in a way the most horrible thing of all. . . .

Ed Troy was a bachelor, and his home was simple enough—a single room for living and eating, one small bedroom, a lean-to at the back for storing food and gear. On a shelf above the stove a cheap tin clock chattered in the stillness, its hands closing on midnight; at the old round dining table, Jim Branch sat alone over the remnants of the meal the liveryman had quickly put together for him, before leaving to do his bit toward cleaning up the last of tonight's dreadful business.

Branch was enjoying a needed smoke and a final cup of coffee when the bedroom door opened and Margie Caufield came out. Closing it carefully behind her, she answered his look with a nod. "Asleep," she said. "And resting well. He'll be all right."

"Of course," Branch said. "It was a clean wound, no bone damage; Troy did as good by it as a lot of doctors could have done. All that's needed is for Wes to take it easy, and let it mend."

He would have risen but the girl stopped him with a lifted hand. She came and took a chair, and placed her folded hands on the table before her. She was still dressed as he'd seen her at the stack yard, in jeans and shirt and flat-topped hat—she'd been awake when the messenger Ed Troy sent from town arrived at Seven Cross, with the word of her brother's injury. She said, "Jim? What about yourself?"

"It was nothing worth mentioning. A strip of court plaster across my ribs took care of it. . . ."

Her eyes searched his face. "I don't suppose you'll tell me why you did it," she said finally. "After what you'd found at the railroad camp, you knew you would be walking into a trap, with the Paxmans and probably some hired gunmen waiting for you in town—yet you said nothing to us at all. It was our battle and you had every right to ask for help. But, I'd told you I didn't want you leading

Wes into a gunfight. And so, you deliberately walked into the thing alone!"

Branch looked at the end of his cigarette; he shrugged uncomfortably. "It was my kind of job, one I was trained for. Anyway, Wes did come in at the last—and a real break for me that he did! He acquitted himself well. He did for Nick Roddy." His eyes challenged the girl's. "Do you think less of your brother, knowing he's killed a man?"

Faint color touched her cheeks but her eyes didn't waver. "You know I don't. I'm proud of him. I'm proud of you both!"

He was the one who looked away. He dropped the cigarette stub into his coffee cup, and abruptly changed the subject. "It'll be some time before the mess the Paxmans made here in the Basin can be straightened out; but at least, with them gone there'll be no one bothering the Seven Cross. You have no more need for a gun. So, don't feel too concerned that your brother may be crippled up for awhile when I leave."

"Meaning," she said, her voice touched with disapproval, "That the gun job you hired to do is finished—and you'll ride on to find another somewhere else, and then another. . . . Jim, that isn't the life for you! I don't believe it! I'm not forgetting Wes told me that you were a rancher, yourself."

"That was some time ago," Jim Branch reminded her. "This is today. A man does what he has to; he goes where his trail leads."

"But yours led to Holster Basin," she pointed out quickly. "Before you ride blindly on again, stop and think for a minute what you yourself just told me: With Vern Paxman gone, this is free range again—and you freed it! Then why shouldn't some of it be yours? Why shouldn't this be the place where you make your start again? I'm not saying it would be easy, but I'm sure your luck would have to be better this time. I know there isn't anyone in the Basin who wouldn't do what he could to help!"

He stared at her a long minute. He started to speak, had to try again. "I won't deny I've been sitting here, thinking along those very lines. But—I don't know. I mean—" He had to put it bluntly, because he knew no other way. "Do you really know what you're saying? Are you sure you want someone like me for a neighbor?"

Suddenly her eyes seemed misted. "Jim Branch, you can't be much of a gentleman," she cried, half laughing and half in earnest. "To make a girl apologize for things she'd rather die than have to admit she said! But if I have to, then I'll do it!" Her warm, competent hand slipped impulsively into his. "I *am* sorry, Jim. And I want you to stay!"

In the stillness the clock on the shelf kept up its mindless chatter, inexorably rattling out the minutes of a man's life. But suddenly it was no melancholy sound. Life was short, and mortality inescapable; yet, with courage, a man had it in his power to give meaning to the time that was allowed him, and not merely go drifting aimlessly down the years. Perhaps, even for Jim Branch, it wasn't yet too late.

He didn't try to put any of this in words. He returned the pressure of the girl's fingers that lay in his own, and smiled at her as he nodded.

D(wight) B(ennett) Newton is the author of a number of notable Western novels. Born in Kansas City, Missouri, Newton went on to complete work for a Master's degree in history at the University of Missouri. From the time he first discovered Max Brand in Street and Smith's *Western Story Magazine,* he knew he wanted to be an author of Western fiction. He began contributing Western stories and novelettes to the Red Circle group of Western pulp magazines published by Newsstand in the late 1930s. During the Second World War, Newton served in the US Army Engineers and fell in love with the central Oregon region when stationed there. He would later become a permanent resident of that state and Oregon frequently serves as the locale for many of his finest novels. As a client of the August Lenniger Literary Agency, Newton found that every time he switched publishers he was given a different byline by his agent. This complicated his visibility. Yet in notable novels from *Range Boss* (1949), the first original novel ever published in a modern paperback edition, through his impressive list of titles for the Double D series from Doubleday, *The Oregon Rifles, Crooked River Canyon,* and *Disaster Creek* among them, he produced a very special kind of Western story. What makes it so special is the combination of characters who seem real and about whom a reader comes to care a great deal and Newton's fundamental humanity, his realization early on (perhaps because of his study of history) that little that happened in the West was ever simple but rather made desperately complicated through the conjunction of numerous opposed forces working at cross purposes. Yet, through all of the turmoil on the frontier, a basic human decency did emerge. It was this which made the American frontier experience so profoundly unique and which produced many of the remarkable human beings to be found in the world of Newton's Western fiction.